Chayalocha

Chayalocha

by ShanE Johnson

BARBOUR
PUBLISHING

© 2003 by Shane Johnson

ISBN 1-59310-051-5

Scripture quotations are taken from the King James Version of the Bible.

This book is a work of fiction. Names, characters, places, and incidents are either products of the author's imagination or used fictitiously. Any similarity to actual people, organizations, and/or events is purely coincidental.

Cover image © Index Stock.

The author is represented by Alive Communications Inc., 7680 Goddard Street, Suite 200, Colorado Springs, CO 80920.

Published by Barbour Publishing, Inc., P.O. Box 719, Uhrichsville, Ohio 44683, www.barbourbooks.com

Our mission is to publish and distribute inspirational products offering exceptional value and biblical encouragement to the masses.

ecpa Member of the
Evangelical Christian
Publishers Association

Printed in the United States of America.

5 4 3 2 1

DEDICATION

For Steve McClellan

A dear friend, my best friend,
who departed this life in July of 2002.

For twenty–seven years,
I knew the privilege of his company.
Though for now we are separated,
I will hear his laugh again.

Prologue

April 1797

The hawk circled, lost for a moment in the glare of the warm, loving sun.

A little boy, squinting upward as he sat cross-legged near the cooking fire, watched the large, dark bird as it rode the clear sky. Its mastery of the air amazed him, drawing forth longings he felt each new day as the young braves around him played their games, as they embarked on the hunt with their fathers, spears in hand, sharing in the ways of their ancestors.

Longings he felt, born of disparity, of loneliness.

If only I could be up there with you. . .

If only. . .

Looking down at his club foot, he tucked it more tightly beneath himself, as if ashamed.

If only I could run and hunt and do so many other things.

The medicine man had done his best, yet to no avail. The foot was no better.

Why must I be different?

The valley stretched wide around him, a tapestry of lush meadows, sparkling waters, and lofty trees whose branches sang to the slightest breezes. On all sides, hazed by distance, towered a wreath of snowcapped mountains, almost impenetrable, forging at their feet a paradise hidden from the rest of the world.

And protected from it.

The village rested along the shore of a small, tranquil lake, a liquid canvas that mirrored the purples, blues, and whites of the surrounding peaks. The boy smiled as a fish broke the surface, hinting at the ample bounty below. The subtle, widening rings cast by the splash lapped gently just a few feet away, inviting the boy for a cool swim.

Forests of tall firs and cedars rose near the shoreline and into the distance, sentries that gave themselves for homes, canoes, hunting implements, and totem poles. Dozens of the massive totems were arrayed throughout the village, guarding the history of the people, telling their tales to any who could read their design. The stand of trees also gave shelter to an abundance of wild game and fur-bearing animals, a provision of meat for the tribe's stomachs and skins for their clothing and rugs.

The scent of corn wafted on white wisps of steam rising from an iron pot, one of many gifts to the tribe brought by French traders, newcomers to the land. The boy watched as the women of the village tended to their tasks, preparing the midday meal and watching over the younger children.

They were the Welakiutl. Never had they known attack, or

famine, or pestilence. For centuries, there in that place, they had lived out their lives, happily leaving the land beyond the mountains to other tribes, from whom they were descended.

The boy turned as a friendly, familiar voice called out to him.

"Good morning, little one." The bearded man smiled, speaking in the child's native tongue.

"Good morning!"

"Parlez vous Francais?" the man teased, knowing well the answer.

"Oui! " replied the boy, grinning. Their conversation continued in French. "You slept well?"

"Indeed." The fur-clothed trader nodded, adjusting his wide leather belt. "But then, I always do when I come to this place. A little slice of heaven it is, here on earth." He knelt and ran his hand gently through the boy's thick mane of black hair. "You speak my language well. . .as well as my own son. . . "

"Jacques." The boy smiled, remembering.

"Yes," the trader said, nodding, seeing his own child in the boy's dark eyes and missing him terribly. "In a few months I'll be with him again. I'll tell him of you. . .of how proud I am of you, and how quickly you learn. It is a pity the two of you cannot meet. You would be great friends, I think."

He rose again to his feet and surveyed the village. He was a frequent visitor, usually spending weeks at a time, and he was well known within the tribe, a friend.

The man waved to the boy's mother, who knelt a few yards away, cleaning fish from an earlier catch. She smiled and returned the greeting, then called out to her son, telling him not to make a nuisance of himself.

"He is a delight," the trader answered her in Welakiutl. Then, to the boy, in French, "I must be leaving soon. The western outpost is waiting. But I'll pass near here again as I return home, and

I'll spend a night or two."

"I will miss you." The boy frowned.

"And I will miss my star pupil." The man reached into a pocket and pulled out a small timepiece. "Here," he said, placing it into the child's hand. "I showed you what the hands mean, yes? And how to keep it wound?"

"*Oui, monsieur.*" He nodded, his eyes going wide as he looked upon the shiny silver object.

"This is yours. I picked it up from a kind gentleman back home, in Lower Canada. . ."

"In Trois-Rivières," the boy piped up.

"Yes." The trader grinned, pulling a second watch, this one layered in gold, from a different pocket. "I have another, see? A gift from my wife."

"Marie."

"You know everything about me." The man laughed. "Perhaps I should have spoken more carefully. No matter, little one. The watch is yours. You can use it to count the minutes until again we meet."

"*Merci,*" the boy said, holding the ticking prize to his ear. A new smile crossed his face.

They started across the village common, where children played as the women and older men went about their business. The trader stopped occasionally to speak to some of the men, taking notes for future trades. The limping boy stayed close at his side, watching, listening, and learning.

From the fields in the distance, joyous whoops faintly sounded—the hunt was going well.

"Quite a feast we'll have tonight, no?" said the trader, patting his stomach and smiling as the boy did the same. "Heaven on earth. . ."

A new wind filled the trees. Gentle at first, it rose quickly.

The birds went quiet, then took to the skies in a rush of swift, dark motion.

Like an ocean wave, a deep cold swept the village, rolling in from across the lake. The howling in the trees intensified. The temperature plunged as the warmth of the sun fled away.

"Odd," the trader whispered, turning his gaze toward the snowy peaks, his breath going white. "Something coming down off the mountain. . . ?"

Panic swept the tribe and they began to run, their fearful utterances filling the chilled air. The boy turned and hobbled toward his mother, but he was knocked to the ground more than once as the crowd scrambled in all directions. Seeing him fall, the woman hurried to his side and led him clear of the frenzy.

Above the valley a darkness coalesced, drawing itself out of nothing. Like a colossal hand it descended, rapidly widening, usurping the sun.

Most of the frightened villagers sought shelter, but a few stood in stunned amazement, squinting into the gale as they watched the shadow drop upon them. The boy and his mother took refuge at the entrance to their cedar-planked home, clinging helplessly to each other in the biting cold.

The light died away. The faint remnants of springtime blue that lingered at the periphery above blackened to midnight—but there were no stars, no moon.

Nothing.

Screams erupted in the distance, punctuating the roar of the wind as they rose from amid the hunting fields. Cries of agony, both human and animal, each in turn going silent with terrifying suddenness. Then, closer, came the wrenching crack of massive tree trunks, twisting and splintering where they stood.

"Inside!" the trader cried out. "Everyone!"

The trembling boy clung to his mother, barely able to see her. He began to cry as again and again she called out into the darkness, seeking a reassuring reply from the boy's father. Her words sounded odd, seemingly smothered as they left her lips.

The boy felt the hard, black air as it pressed heavily against his skin, coating his nostrils with a thick, unyielding iciness. He tried to wipe it away but his hands found nothing there, nothing his fingers could touch.

He felt himself being dragged backward and through the doorway of the house. Unable now to see, he heard the slam of the door and the sound of his mother weeping—her voice low as she repeated the name of his father. Her unsteady footsteps crossed the room.

"Mother," the boy called out, still crying. "What is—"

He was silenced and startled by a crash, a clatter of metal and wood.

"Mother!"

"I am here, Seukani. . . ."

A moment later, the glow of a lantern filled the room, though it did not flare as brightly as it should have. The small table where his mother prepared food lay on its side, knives and cooking utensils littering the floor around it.

"What happened outside?" he asked, not at all certain that his mother would know the answer. "Has winter not passed?"

His mother lowered herself onto a plush, animal hide rug and beckoned to him, her tears glistening in the faint light. Drawing an unsteady breath and wiping his eyes, Seukani went to her, his cold-numbed arms finding comfort as they slipped around her waist. She draped a blanket around them both, and in the soft golden light they sat together, sharing their warmth, drawing strength from each other.

● ● ●

"Mother? I do not understand. . .the dark. . .the cold. . . "

"He has come," the woman whispered to herself, her words rising in chilled white wisps, her voice heavy with dread.

"Who has come?"

She turned, realizing she had been overheard. Her eyes darted as she considered the question, debating whether to answer.

Her gaze fell to the floor. Gently, she caressed the child's bare forearm, remembering the tiny infant he once had been. Slowly, deliberately, she spoke a name, one the boy had never heard.

"Ky-a-toe-ka."

"What?"

"Chayatocha," she repeated.

"I don't understand. . . ."

She thought better of telling him. Frightening her son would change nothing—already, it was too late.

"Never mind," she replied, trying her best to appear unconcerned. "It is just an old story, one our ancestors used to tell. When your father returns from the hunt, you may ask him about it."

Her words were hollow. She had heard the screams.

She held the boy close, cradling his head, stroking his hair. In the near darkness they sat, listening to the howl of the wind outside, the creaking of the house as it stood against the icy gale.

The ancient legends were true—

"Do not be afraid," she reassured him, gently rocking him as she fought to disguise her own fear. "I am here, and we are together, and we are safe."

But they were not, she knew.

Finally, he has come—to devour the world.

Chapter 1

Sixty Years Later

The sun.

The unrelenting sun.

Daniel Paradine adjusted the brim of his hat and gazed upward, squinting in the glare as his eyes followed the lazy course of a buzzard circling high in the distance. The cloudless sky stretched on as it had for weeks, vast and blue, draped upon the wilderness around him. Mountains rose on the far horizon, their whitened tops obscured by the distance.

The steady rumble of wooden wheels filled the air, punctuated by the creaks and groans of the wagon forks and the pounding rhythm of hooves against the hard, baked soil. The sound of dozens of worn leather boots and shoes joined the percussion as they treaded the unforgiving ground.

Paradine momentarily removed his spectacles and wiped their lenses clean with a handkerchief. The pervasive dust was always a problem. Seeing more clearly now, he looked down at the trail, at the wheel ruts etched by thousands of wagons over more than a dozen years. He drew a measure of comfort from their constant presence.

If those folks made it, so can we.

He watched his livestock as they pulled the blue-trimmed prairie schooner he had purchased for his family. Large enough to haul cargo but small enough not to exhaust the beasts pulling it, the wagon carried everything he still owned. The half-dozen oxen were the healthiest he could find in all of Independence, Missouri, the starting point for this cross-continental journey. As with many pioneers, Paradine and his family had named the beasts—the largest was Willy, followed by Hugo, Clementine, Sam, Uncle Aloysius, and Clyde—and for now, they were like members of the family. But he and the others held no illusions about the animals' true place. In the event of a crisis, none would be exempt from the butcher's blade.

If it came to that.

Tomorrow held no promises, he knew, and never had, but odds were they would complete their crossing. Onward they pressed, into the Oregon Territory—twelve wagons filled with optimism, their axles burdened by as many personal belongings as had been deemed safe. Twelve wagons headed west, toward new lands and new lives.

Twelve fragile wagons, three score oxen, sixteen horses, seventeen cattle, a dozen mules, and fifty-three souls sustained by rationed food, measured water, and unbounded aspirations.

An inventory of hope, carried upon dreams.

Paradine's ankles ached. Those fit enough to walk did so, while the few who were too old or injured to maintain the pace traveled on horseback. No one rode in the wagons—the heavily laden schooners presented enough of a burden to the oxen without the added weight of passengers. Fashioned of hickory, maple, or oak, with iron used sparingly and only where its strength was vital, they had been built as sturdily as possible while remaining relatively lightweight.

A glint of polished wood caught Paradine's eye. He turned to see a once-prized china hutch lying in the grass, only a few feet from the rutted trail. Its glass doors had shattered, but its rich red finish had not yet succumbed to the elements. Those who had abandoned it had passed this way only recently.

Paradine knew that as their own oxen wearied, his group might well be forced to jettison some of their heavier possessions. Hundreds of times along the trail they had seen ornate furniture, musical instruments, and all manner of personal property left behind, its value weighed against the odds of survival and found wanting.

My books—

They were the reason for his journey.

They must be spared!

Back home, Paradine and his family had owned one of the largest personal libraries in their small Ohio town. He was well liked, and his job as a schoolteacher had brought with it a modest level of local notoriety. He and his family had been comfortable, though by no means wealthy, living their lives each day in anticipation of a tomorrow filled with greater opportunity.

One day, as a literal knock on the door, it had come.

Paradine glanced to his right, where his wife and eight-year-old son made their way along the uneven track, clearly as tired as he was. He remembered how excited Lisabeth had been the morning the telegram had arrived—an invitation from a small municipality on the Willamette River in the Oregon Territory, asking Paradine to found a school *and* a public library. On the recommendation of a former student and her family, who now lived in the fledgling community, the town council of Saraleah had promised him a comfortable house, a dependable job—and the fulfillment of a lifelong dream.

Still, the decision had not been easy. To leave friends and family behind, along with most of their possessions, and travel thousands of miles across open country would be dangerous—sickness, flooding rivers, inclement weather, and hostile attacks might well await them along the way. Many others had died making the trip.

But dreams do not die as easily as mere flesh.

Their son, Michael, of course had been a consideration. *Should we take our son away from all he has known? Should we expose him to the risks of the journey? Should we leave him behind, to be cared for in familiar surroundings?* For weeks, Paradine and his wife had debated, bouncing from one side of the issue to the other. Finally, the boy's unbridled enthusiasm for the adventure had helped them make the decision to head west, their family intact. Roots were torn from the earth, packed in trunks, and ultimately placed within the canvas-covered prairie schooner that now cradled their very lives.

"And here we are," he muttered, casting his gaze across the boundless prairie.

"What?" his wife asked, seeing the consternation playing upon his features.

He forced a smile. "Nothing. . .just thinking out loud, I guess."

"I'm thirsty," Michael piped up, his throat audibly dry. "Is it time for water yet?"

Paradine pulled a silver pocket watch from his vest, opened its cover, and nodded. It was one of the few timepieces being carried on the journey. "Close enough," he said, reaching out to playfully jiggle the boy's brown felt hat. "Go easy, though. . .we've got a long way yet to go."

Without breaking stride, he reached down for the bottle he carried in a leather sling he had contrived, pulled its stopper, and handed it to his son, who took a pair of healthy swallows. Paradine passed the bottle to his wife, who gratefully partook before handing it back.

"I miss Fort Bridger," she moaned, "and I never thought I'd be saying *that.*"

Michael shook his head at her mention of the trading post. The place wasn't much to write home about, and never had been. But it had provided them with the best night's sleep they had known in a while, with a hardwood floor, real beds, and a solid roof overhead.

"I miss Independence," the boy chimed in, recalling their first day among the wagons.

"We're about three-fourths of the way to Saraleah," Paradine reassured them both. "Even before we crossed the Snake River, we were in the Oregon Territory. Soon enough, there'll be hot baths and comfortable beds for us all."

"How can it be so hot right now, when it's freezing at night?" Michael wondered aloud. "It wasn't like this at home."

Paradine indicated the peaks well to the north. "The altitude here is a lot greater than Ohio's. At this point, probably a good six thousand feet or so. Not as high as we were, though, when the trail crested at the Continental Divide. Back at the South Pass."

"Where that ice was?"

Only a foot beneath the soil had rested a great, expansive bed of white, defiantly cold even in the summer midday heat. Chopped from the earth, the frozen treasure had provided such joy—pressed against arms and foreheads, melted in parched mouths, or placed to thaw in kegs for later use.

"Yes, there. . .that whole, wide valley. We've come down a ways, but we're still pretty high up. And there are a lot of mountains still ahead—"

He went silent as he noticed something just up the way, only partly obscured within the grasses. After another moment, he recognized its form.

"Michael," he said abruptly, "climb into the wagon and bring me my other hat, will you?"

"Which one?"

"My black one. Be careful, now. . . ."

"You stay clear of those wheels," his mother ordered with a worried tone. "Go around behind."

"I will, Mama," the boy said. "I was going to." He stood for a moment and let the rolling wagon pass, then climbed aboard at the rear, disappearing beneath the heavy canvas cover.

Lisabeth looked toward her husband. "Couldn't that have waited until we stopped?" She paused as the realization hit, her expression one of increasing puzzlement. "Daniel, you don't *have* a black hat."

His response was a subtle nod ahead. Lisabeth followed his gaze, then gasped as her eyes fell upon an all-too-common horror. She looked away, breathing deeply, her hand to her forehead.

Barely a dozen feet from the trail lay the body of a woman,

contorted and decaying. Her stained cotton sundress was in tatters, her long, tangled hair still auburn and shiny. Just beyond the corpse, an open, shallow grave had been cut into the earth, marked by a crude wooden marker which now lay almost on its side. Upon its uneven surface were scrawled a few simple words:

CHARLOTTE BAKER
BELOVED WIFE AND MOTHER
DIED OF THE CHOLERA
JUNE 1857

Paradine read the epitaph with great sadness. *Just a few months ago, she was alive and well, making her way like the rest of us—*

Many such graves had been left behind, all along the route. They littered the trailside, each telling the story of one who had set out with high hopes, yet had not lived to see their fulfillment. Cholera had taken tens of thousands, having moved up the Mississippi from New Orleans, before spreading west. In some places, entire cemeteries beside the trail gave mute and somber testimony to the plague's virulence. Most victims had perished east of the Divide, yet a few individuals, exposed to the disease later in the journey, had held on longer.

The woman had been buried by her family, but not deep enough. Animals—wolves, most likely—had dug into the soft ground and uncovered her. And they had been hungry.

"Dear Father, bless that poor woman and her family," Lisabeth whispered to herself. "Wherever they are. . .whoever they are. . .in Jesus' name, bring them comfort. . . ."

Everyone in the party went silent upon seeing the body, averting their eyes in respect, never slowing their pace.

"I can't find it," Michael's voice came, stark in the reverent

21

silence yet muffled by the wagon's bonnet.

"Look in the little trunk," Paradine called out, stalling him. "The green one."

"Yes, sir. . .but I'm not sure I can reach it."

"Which ones *can* you reach? Try those."

As the last wagon passed the body, two men with shovels stepped clear of the moving procession and walked somberly back to the disturbed grave, leading a pair of saddled horses.

"Thank you." Paradine nodded to one of the men, Harvey Langtree, as he passed.

"Least we can do," he replied. "Won't take too long. . .we'll catch up before you know it."

"Be careful."

"Surest thing you know."

Another few seconds and they were clear. No longer was the body in view.

"Never mind, son," Paradine called. "I'll just keep the one I'm wearing."

Michael emerged, dropped from the back of the wagon, and ran to rejoin his parents. "I'm sorry," he said.

"Don't be." His father smiled, placing an arm around the boy's shoulder. "Come to think of it, I may have left it back at Fort Laramie. No matter. . .I'm sure they'll have plenty of hats for sale where we're going."

"Nice black ones," Lisabeth added.

◎ ◎ ◎

Shadows grew long as the sun drew near the horizon.

Weariness had taken its toll upon the travelers, as it did each day. Some began to doze on their feet, even as they continued to plod forward. Feet, legs, and hips cried out in protest. It had been a good day—another twenty miles or more had been put behind them.

At the sound of a trumpet, joy filled many a worn-out soul. A welcome routine, now well practiced, would end the day.

Following the lead of the pilot ahead, the men guided the yoked oxen away from the trail, directing their wagons onto a spacious, level area of short grasses. Unable to turn sharply, they curved wide, tightening their formation before coming to rest in a nearly perfect circle that would provide some measure of protection in the event of an attack.

In less than half an hour, the sun fell behind the mountains, and a deep shadow began to descend. At each wagon, a cooking fire was ignited, fueled by sun-dried buffalo chips that had been gathered along the way. The glow of the flames splashed a dance of gold against the sides of the wagons.

Paradine emerged from beneath the canvas cover of his prairie schooner, caught a familiar scent in the air, and climbed down.

"Mmmm-mmmm," Paradine said with a hint of sarcasm, peering into the three-legged skillet. "Buffalo steak. Nothing like it."

"Well, enjoy it while you can," his wife smiled, wiping her hands on her well-used cotton apron.

"I'm tired of it, too, but good meat is good meat."

"Once we get to Saraleah, I'm never cooking this again. No buffalo, no fried cakes, no soda bread. I've had my fill of it."

"Once we get there," he returned, "you'll never have to." He glanced into an open food chest. "How are the supplies holding out?"

"Fine, for now. We'll need to pick up a few things at the next post, though."

"We will."

"We have butter, by the way," Lisabeth said. "I put some milk in the churn, and the rough ride took care of it as we went along."

"Good thinking," her husband smiled.

"I got the idea from Martha Potter, so I can't take full credit."

"A good steak, bread and butter. . .a man could do a lot worse. Good thing the hunting went so well last Thursday. They had to go out a good distance from the trail to find anything, but it was the best day we'd seen in a while."

"Be nice if there was more wildlife closer to the trail," Lisabeth said. "As long as they weren't grizzlies, or anything else that would try to eat us before we ate them."

"Wagon trains tend to make a lot of noise as they pass through. . .scares off most animals. And all the oxen and cattle that people bring with them keep the trailside grasses eaten down. Not much left for the elk, or the deer, or anything else, so they stay away."

"I wish the same were true of the scavengers. It's so frightening to look out there at night and see the eyes of wolves glowing in the lantern light."

Lisabeth turned the steak, then rose and called out. Several children, her son among them, played quietly near one of the other wagons. "Michael," she called out, "time for supper!"

The boy came running, though not as quickly as he might have had he not been on his feet most of the day. Paradine rubbed him on the head as he passed, then looked across the circular camp, toward the lead wagon on the other side.

Something was happening. And from the looks of it, it was not good.

The leader of the wagon train, a burly former cavalry officer named Jeremiah Wills, stood surveying their surroundings with several other men. All bore upon their hardened faces expressions of deep concern.

"I'll be right back," Paradine said, as the others began to dish out their meals. He headed across the grass, not knowing whether he could help to solve the problem but willing to try. The drone of the field crickets was steady, but not so loud that he heard nothing else—as he neared the men, he realized they were speaking in low tones, not wishing to be overheard.

"Could be real trouble. . .if his report's half reliable, we—"

As Paradine approached the group, the men went silent.

"Captain," the schoolteacher said in greeting, the tension around him palpable.

"Mr. Paradine."

"Is there a problem?"

"Nothing we can't handle," said a wiry, hatchet-faced man at Wills' side, a measure of derision in his voice. He scratched at his long, scraggly beard. "You just go back to your books, and leave things to us."

There it was again.

"Hello, Mr. Garrett," Paradine said flatly, noting the man's filthy clothes and level of personal hygiene—low even for such a journey. "I want to thank you for doing your best to assure the rest of us an ample supply of water."

The remark, on razor's wings, sailed directly over the man's head.

"There'll be enough," the puzzled man gruffly replied. "Gonna have to go easy, though. It's a long way yet to Fort Boise."

Paradine felt the eyes upon him, taking note of his brocade vest and glittering watch fob, the silver rims of his eyeglasses, and his manicured fingernails. All those things, he knew, were seen by some as alien, even threatening or undeserving of respect.

Chayalocha

Perhaps that disrespect also grew out of the way he moved and the vocabulary he used, reflecting his refined upbringing and learned mind.

Almost since leaving Missouri, Paradine had detected a growing tension when interacting with a handful of the party's men. It was nothing new—all his life he had felt like something of an outsider, and in his younger days he had suffered as the continual target of bullies, loudmouths, and anyone else out to prove a point. Unlike most every other boy he knew, he was given to literary studies and an appreciation of the arts, rather than to the more rough-and-tumble dealings of everyday life.

"I just wanted to lend assistance."

Wills gestured back in the direction from which Paradine had come. "I appreciate that, Teacher, but like the man said, you needn't worry."

"What's the problem?"

"We don't need a dandy stickin' his nose in," Garrett said.

"That'll do, Asa," Wills said, backhanding the man's chest. "Go get Johnny and tell him I want to see him."

Without further word, Garrett turned his back and crossed between the wagons. Following a subtle motion of the wagon master's head, the other men dispersed, leaving Wills and Paradine standing alone.

"Asa don't mean no harm," the captain said. "Barely thirteen when his father died. . .worked on the family farm most of his life, trying to support his mother and sisters. He never got any formal schooling. I reckon he's a bit envious of you, in his way."

"I don't mind him."

"Good man, really. . .ornery as the day is long, but a good man."

"So, what did I walk up on?" Paradine repeated.

"I know you've got a well-educated brain there, Mr. Paradine,

26

and to be honest, I'd appreciate your opinion right about now."

"Anything I can do."

"I'm sure you heard about Johnny coming back this morning."

"I heard." Paradine nodded, having been told of the scout's arrival. "But only that he'd returned."

"Don't spread this around," Wills began, "but he brought back word of an Indian attack up the trail a piece. Another day's travel ahead." The man scowled, as if questioning.

"What is it? What did he say?"

Wills shook his head. "Man came back kinda funny. Hard to get a handle on, exactly, but. . ."

"What did he see?"

"Said there were some burned wagons up there, and a lot of dead folks and slaughtered cattle. So he says."

"You don't believe him?"

"Can't afford *not* to. Problem is, if something's wrong with him, if the sun got to him or he's coming down sick or is out of his head, and we leave the trail in order to avoid Indians, we could wind up lost, or worse." He cast a glance between the wagons, toward the west and the fading orange sky. "Doc says he seems fine, except for. . .well, he ain't running a fever or nothing. In fact, just the opposite."

"What do you mean?"

The scout appeared as if on cue, approaching slowly, his eyes untrusting. To Paradine, he seemed almost like a wild animal, uncomfortable in the presence of man.

"Johnny," the captain began, wary of the glassy look in the man's eyes, "you know Daniel Paradine?"

No answer came, but the scout instinctively offered a hand. Paradine took it.

It was cold, as if the man had just climbed out of a winter pond.

It's got to be eighty degrees out here.

Paradine looked at Wills, who raised a knowing eyebrow. Returning his gaze to the scout, he broke the handshake and rubbed his chilled fingers together.

"You get some sleep, Johnny?" the wagon master asked. "We were worried about you."

"I'm fine," the scout said.

"You eat?" Wills persisted.

"I'm fine."

"How sure are you of what you saw out there?"

"Told you what I saw," the scout said quietly, looking away.

"How do you know it was Indians who killed them?" Paradine asked. "Not robbers, or—"

"Dead one, left behind," the man cut in, never making eye contact. "Under a wagon. Half burned up."

"How recently did it happen? The attack, I mean."

"Within the week. . .they're sure to be up there, somewhere."

"How would you suggest we bypass them?" the teacher asked.

The scout turned his head sharply to the northwest and stared, despite the fact that his view of the horizon was blocked by the wagon immediately behind him. "Found a pass. . .cuts through the mountains. Narrow, but it opens up after a bit. Good place to camp, if need be. Should make for easy goin'. Won't lose more than a couple days, at most."

Wills, visibly uncertain, exchanged a worried glance with Paradine before lightly patting the enigmatic scout on the back. "Okay, Johnny. You get some supper, and try to sleep through the night. Four's gonna come early."

Without another word, the man turned and slunk away.

"Odd," Paradine noted. "He's never acted this way before?"

"Nope."

"Well, perhaps he—"

"That ain't the weirdest part," Wills continued, removing his hat and scratching his head of thinning hair. "He left with food and water for only two days, but he was gone for *six*. We'd given him up for dead."

"Six *days?* But how far did *we* travel in that time. . .a hundred miles or better?"

"Something like that."

"How could he survive out there for that long?"

"Wasn't a bit of his provisions on him when he got back. In fact, he was missing his pack altogether. Didn't even have his rifle. Don't know how he made it. Better question is, how did he find us again? Just came walking up this morning, as casual as you like, as if nothing was wrong, as if he knew exactly where we'd be. It was a miracle, plain and simple. . . . A needle in a haystack woulda been child's play next to that."

"Wait a minute," Paradine said, his brow furrowed in disbelief. "*Walking?*"

"Came back without his horse. When we asked him where it went, he just shook his head and repeated over and over that there are Indians out there."

"So, what do we do?"

"Ask me again tomorrow," the wagon master replied. "I might know by then."

Chapter 2

The rifles did not fire.

Each morning since their journey had begun, at precisely four o'clock, fragments of lead had thundered high into the air. That signal served as a wakeup call, sharply and insistently heralding the new day.

But not *this* day.

As the cobwebs cleared, Paradine realized he was being shaken from his sleep by a crouching Gordon Quonset, one of the half-dozen sentinels who kept watch through the night.

"Time to get started," the man said, leaning into the tent. "You awake?"

"Yes," Paradine mumbled, recalling at once his situation, there with his family, under their heavy blankets and atop their ground cloths. Propping himself on one elbow, he ran a hand through his tousled hair. "I'm up."

Convinced, the man nodded and rose. "Havin' a meeting promptly at seven, at the center of camp. Everyone's included."

"Okay," Paradine said, still bleary-eyed. "We'll be there."

Quonset walked away, headed for another wagon, another sleepy family. Some folks slept inside their wagons, but for the Paradines, with their load of books and other necessities, sleeping inside was not an option.

Paradine sat up, rubbed his eyes, and lit the small lantern, keeping its light low. Out of habit, he checked his pocket watch.

Four-twelve.

Reaching over, he roused Lisabeth.

"Why no rifle shots?" the woman asked, her eyes still closed.

"I'm sure they have their reasons," Paradine replied, recalling the scout's report. He did not wish to alarm his wife unnecessarily when he might not have all the facts. "Meeting at seven, he said. I suppose they'll tell us something then."

"So cold," Lisabeth said, visibly reluctant to emerge from her blankets. "How I miss those first few nights, just outside Missouri."

"Look how far we've come." Her husband smiled. "Not much farther now."

"How nice it will be to be back in a house again. I'll never complain about mopping floors or washing windows as long as I live."

"I'm going to hold you to that."

"Just because I'm not complaining doesn't mean you won't be right there helping me."

"I wouldn't have it any other way."

"I hope it's yellow. . . ."

"What is?" Paradine asked.

"Our house," Lisabeth said. "Yellow with white trim. . .with a white picket fence and flower beds surrounding a stone walk."

"You're describing that house on Donovan Street. . .the one we looked at before Michael was born."

"I loved that house."

He bent down and kissed her tenderly, then reached across and shook his son gently out of his slumber.

"Morning, son."

The boy slurred something unintelligible in response. Paradine chuckled.

"I'll have him up," Lisabeth said. "He's never missed a breakfast yet."

Knowing his son was in good hands, the teacher emerged from the tent and stretched to his full height.

As he stood watching in his flannel nightshirt and trousers, all around him the other travelers returned to life. Lanterns glowed and danced as they were carried by their owners. Chickens clucked within their coops slung on the sides of most of the wagons. Kindling was ignited, bringing on the warmth, gentle light, and wisps of smoke of the cooking fires. The scent of strong coffee wafted through the cold air. Mules brayed until their nagging was rewarded with a feedbag. In the distance, Paradine heard but could not see the oxen and horses, all voicing their familiar protests as they were driven from the surrounding grassland and closer to camp. Low, gentle strains of violin music wafted from somewhere across the way.

That would be the Donovan boy. He sure knows how to treat Bach, for one so young.

Paradine reflected on the challenges the party had faced along the way. He thought of the wagons—and the lives—that had been lost. The Pruitt family, who had lost their three young children to drowning when their wagon had tipped over during a river crossing. The Calloways, who had broken an axle and then watched helplessly as their wagon had tumbled down a steep hillside, splintering against the rocks at the bottom. Fortunately, no one had died in that mishap, but all of the family's possessions had been lost.

All in all, however, it had been a successful journey. Four people had died—the Pruitt children and a man who had slipped in the mud and had fallen under the wheels of his wagon—but disease had played no real role in the journey, and the injuries for the most part had been minor. For that they were all thankful. Their supplies, carefully meted out, were lasting well, and the hunting had been good enough to keep them in roasted meats and jerky. Only a few oxen had been lost, and those that had perished had provided further sustenance for the travelers.

Mechanical troubles had been surprisingly rare, with only a few broken wagon wheels. The storms they had encountered had not been severe, with no lightning strikes, flash floods, or hail—all of which could be lethal.

It was well known that many of the hundreds of thousands who had attempted the cross-country trek never had reached their destinations, falling victim to any number of perils along the way. Some of the victims had been discovered by later wagon trains, but the fate of many more remained a mystery.

Combing his hair with his fingers, Paradine peered upward and felt the same awe he always knew when beholding the heavens. There was no moon, and the sun had not yet begun its ascent, leaving millions of brilliant stars to twinkle in the velvet blackness.

Such beauty—so infinite, so unreachable.

He turned and reentered the tent, where he found his wife

and son reading from the Bible, as was their way each morning and night.

"*. . .and I will pray the Father,*" the woman read, as the boy looked on. "*And he shall give you another Comforter, that he may abide with you forever. . . .*"

She glanced up at her husband, paused, and then continued.

"*Even the Spirit of truth; whom the world cannot receive, because it seeth him not, neither knoweth him. . .but ye know him, for he dwelleth in you, and shall be in you.*"

Daniel Paradine neither saw nor knew the Spirit to whom she referred. He'd never had much time for religion, and he'd been none too happy when Lisabeth had begun attending the tiny whitewashed church in their hometown. But her newfound beliefs seemed innocuous enough, and he allowed her faith to grow without complaint, even as she brought their young son into the fold. Her attempts to draw her husband nearer to faith in God had failed. He felt no need for the emotional "crutch" and had always considered religion a sign of intellectual weakness.

Of course, Paradine knew the Bible backward and forward, verse-by-verse. In fact, he'd read it for years and often used the text in his classroom teachings. After all, it was a great literary work and reliable historical text. But appreciating its literary value and finding the personal inner faith of which it so eloquently spoke were two different things.

Paradine knew the words, but he did not *believe*. For him, the pages of the Bible were as dead as the desiccated mummies of Egypt—relics of a bygone age to be studied, for sure; but, ultimately, they were relics with no real application to the modern world.

But, if it makes them happy to believe in all that, what's the harm?

"Bacon and eggs would hit the spot," he said as Lisabeth closed the book. "Anything I can do to help?"

"Your part comes later." She smiled. "Getting everything back into the wagon."

"Yes, ma'am." He reached for his white cotton shirt.

"We'll have to go easy on the bacon," she mentioned. "I know how much you like it, but we need to be careful. Otherwise, it'll be gone within the week."

"But we had that whole—"

"Had is right," she playfully scolded him, "until *someone* kept tossing extra portions into the skillet each morning."

"Point taken, dearest." He smiled, conceding defeat. "I should have bought a bit more. . .at a penny a pound, you can't go wrong."

"We'll have to remember that for the *next* time we pack up and cross the continent."

He bent down and kissed her. "I love you."

"I love you, too."

"Remember. . .meeting's at seven. We'll need to be ready to leave by then."

"We will be, darling," she assured him, handing the Bible to Michael, who in turn placed it into a small wooden chest that held several family treasures. "We always are."

◉ ◉ ◉

Some things never change, even in the middle of nowhere.

Looking into a small hand mirror, Paradine dragged a straight razor upward under his chin, the last stroke of the morning. He swirled the blade in the cloudy, speckled water of his porcelain shaving bowl, dried it with a cloth, and folded it shut. With a small towel he wiped the remaining traces of shaving soap from his face, and he was done.

Just because I have to travel like a mountain man, he mused, taking a final glance in the mirror, *doesn't mean I have to look like one.*

The sun had broken over the horizon, and seven o'clock came quickly. Breakfast was over and the cooking fires throughout the camp had been extinguished. Families that had erected tents had struck them, loading the wagons for travel once again. The teams of oxen were yoked, and as several of the travelers checked their animals one last time, a gathering quietly began.

The short grasses moved in waves like water, carried by the chilled breeze. Paradine crossed the camp and came to a stop near the back of the assembled party, his wife and son at his side. Lisabeth took his arm.

"Daniel, what's this about?"

"There was trouble," he softly said. "We may have to alter our plans a little."

"How do you know? What did you hear?"

"Patience, my love."

Captain Wills climbed atop a wooden crate at the center of the congregation and waited a few moments for the remaining stragglers to gather around.

"Okay, folks," he began. "We're about to head out. Likely won't make Fort Boise today, but that's not why I've called this meeting. I'm sure you all suspected we're trying to be a little quiet this morning, seein' as how we did things a bit differently in rousing you.

"As most of you know, we were blessed in having our Johnny return to us yesterday morning. . . . "

There was a murmur within the crowd. Those who had not witnessed the man's miraculous return firsthand certainly had heard of it. "None of you got to speak with him, though, since he was sleeping and all, but I'm afraid what he brought with him was some bad news. There's been an Indian attack up ahead, about a day's travel from here. Snake Indians, most likely, north of the river. Likely we'd be getting there just before it came time to stop and make camp, at a point where we'd all be tired after a hard day."

The crowd reacted, more loudly this time.

"Now, we don't know if the Indians are still around or not. They might've taken what they wanted and headed out."

"What kind of attack?" a man yelled out.

"Took on a few wagons," Wills explained. "It wasn't good. Looks like everyone was killed or captured, and fires were set."

"How *many* wagons?"

"Five."

"They wouldn't attack a full dozen, would they?" another man asked. "I mean, wouldn't they likely let us pass?"

"I ain't about to speak for them," Wills said. "We know they used to ambush wagon trains a lot bigger than ours, a few years back. Haven't done it much lately, but that doesn't mean they *won't.*"

"Maybe we should turn back," one woman said. "Head back to Fort Hall. . ."

"That's almost two hundred miles behind us," came a reply. "We'd lose weeks or more. We'd never reach the coast before winter sets in."

"Better than dying out here in this forsaken place!" the woman insisted.

Wills held his hands up. "Now, now. . .everybody settle down. We're not turning back, and we're not heading into the area where the attack happened."

"What then?" asked more than one.

"Johnny found a mountain pass for us, away from the Indians. That's why he was gone so long. He followed the cutoff through to the other side. Says it would let us steer clear of the trouble ahead."

Everyone looked to the side, toward the scout, who stood leaning against the wheel of a wagon, apparently unconcerned.

"We'd be joining up with the trail again on the other side of Fort Boise," Wills went on, "and wouldn't lose more than a couple days or so. If we have to. . .if we decide our provisions won't last us until Fort Walla Walla. . .we can double back and get at the outpost from the western side. We'd likely lose *another* couple of days that way, but we'd still be ahead of the weather and shouldn't have any problem."

The travelers turned to each other, discussing the pros and cons of each course of action, weighing the risks. The wagon master stood silently, allowing them the time they needed.

"Just whereabouts will we be leaving the trail?" asked a bearded man in a floppy hat. "And how far will we be having to stray from it?"

"About ten miles from here," Wills answered. "As for how far we'll have to go out of our way, could be looking at forty or fifty miles. But better that than having our wagons burned to the ground, or worse."

A general buzz of consent rose from the crowd, and words in support of the plan were spoken by more than a few.

"So, we're in agreement?" Wills asked. "Show of hands for continuing on, but taking the pass Johnny found for us?"

Almost all reached up into the cold morning air.

"All opposed. . .wanting to turn back?"

Three hands went up.

"All for keeping to the trail all the way, and taking our chances that the Indians have moved on, or otherwise won't attack?"

None.

Wills took a deep, cleansing breath, which fogged white as it reemerged from his lips in a string of husky, decisive words. "The pass it is, then. Everyone get set. . .we're moving out."

More than fifty intrepid souls dispersed and turned to the immediate tasks at hand, taking the remaining, well-practiced steps that would put them back on the trail, another hard day before them.

◉ ◉ ◉

The sunlight bore down, glinting upon the crystal of Paradine's watch.

One forty-three, he read, wiping his brow.

"I hope that pass he found is coming soon," he said, stifling a cough as he walked beside his wife. "Judging from what the good captain said, if it takes much longer, it'll likely be dark before we come to a safe stopping place."

"I'm sure it's just ahead, now," Lisabeth assured him, her voice muffled by the linen fabric she held to her mouth and nose as she trudged along the dusty trail.

"Having to go so far out of our way like this," Paradine muttered, doing his best to ignore the pervasive dust. "Blessed Indians. . .nothing but trouble. I heard the British even abandoned Fort Boise because of their attacks. If not for the fur traders, there'd be no one left there to get supplies from."

"Why are they mad?" Michael asked, from just behind.

"Who?"

"The Indians."

40

Paradine considered the question, coughing once or twice before finally giving up and raising his handkerchief to his face. "I suppose they don't like having all these people like us moving through their territory."

"Did we ask first?" the boy wondered.

"I don't know, son."

@ @ @

Wills, with whip in hand, walked alongside the lead wagon. Quonset followed immediately to the left, leading a saddled horse. Up on the driver's seat of the wagon sat Johnny, still looking none too healthy as far as Wills was concerned.

Trusting my life—all our lives—to the word of a man like that.

"Here," the scout suddenly piped up, after hours of morbid silence.

"What's that?" asked the surprised wagon master.

"We head north, here," Johnny repeated, pointing toward the mountains rising vast and purple above the plain about ten miles away.

"You're sure?"

"That's the cutoff," the scout insisted, his voice low and raspy.

Wills and Quonset exchanged glances, then resigned themselves to their chosen course of action. The sentry climbed atop his mount and rode slightly ahead, then came to a stop and turned, blocking the trail. With a repeating gesture he indicated the new, northward course.

The lead wagon, under Wills' guidance, pulled right and left the trail, cutting across the virgin plain. Quonset continued to wave, guiding the others to follow as one by one they departed the beaten path.

Please, Wills hoped, *let him not be crazy.*

The thick, short grass subdued the sound of their wheels. The dust ceased, much to everyone's delight, and the softer terrain was cooler against the soles of their feet.

Soon, the harsh and heavily traveled Oregon Trail fell behind them and vanished from sight.

◎ ◎ ◎

Ahead, carved between the massive, snow-peaked upthrusts of rock that were the northern Rockies, lay the one safe route their scout had promised they would find.

Please, Paradine hoped, *don't let that man be out of his mind.*

He paused to clean the dust from his glasses, that he might better study the peaks rising before them: impressive and powerful and seemingly impassable. Yet there at the base of the foothills, or so the scout had claimed, lay the path to salvation.

For hours, the mountains seemed unchanging, as if the travelers were drawing no closer. Scattered rocks of increasing size and frequency appeared as they drove onward, forcing the wagons to take a slower, more careful course as they steered clear.

The sun would not wait. It dropped lower in the sky, threatening to leave too soon and rob the pioneers of the light they needed. Too much time was slipping away, and still the pass lay far ahead.

We'll be setting up camp in the dark, Paradine worried. *Won't get the lay of the land, won't get to choose our spot.*

He checked his watch again.

Almost sundown.

Suddenly, it seemed, the mountains loomed ominously above,

their uppermost crests hidden by high clouds, their ravines and treacherous slopes shouting a silent warning. Huge boulders blocked the way to either side, as if funneling the procession onto a set path.

The pass lay open before them.

Paradine gazed up at the sheer cliffs on either side. He saw no sign of an earlier wagon passage, no initials carved into the stone, no painted signs or arrows. Nothing. *Are we the first ones to come this way?*

Well, at least there was no evidence of an Indian presence.

Not that they'd leave signs. . .

Wary of an ambush from above, the wagon train pressed forward into the divide, dwarfed by the enormity of the surrounding rocks. Then men and beasts, women and children, wagons and worldly possessions disappeared, as if the earth itself had swallowed them alive.

◉ ◉ ◉

Wills strained to see ahead, but the increasing shadows dimmed the narrow canyon, prompting some to light lanterns.

"Johnny, you sure this widens up ahead?" he asked. "If it's a box canyon, or—"

"Yes," the scout promised, his eyes closed. "Widens."

The groans and squeaks of the wagons echoed from the faces of the rock, yet the travelers themselves remained silent in awe and trepidation. The heat of the day rapidly fell away, and the cold began to settle in.

Still they rolled as the sky above darkened from purple to royal to midnight blue.

◎ ◎ ◎

Paradine, his wife fearfully grasping his arm, felt more uncertain with every passing moment.

This pass has to open up soon—someplace we can make camp. It has to!

And then the blackness became total. The sun was gone. The only light they had was that which they carried with them.

The party pressed on, holding lanterns aloft or hanging them from hooks on the fronts of the wagons. Eerie shadows played on the sides of the canyon until, suddenly—to everyone's relief—the walls fell away altogether and the pass widened, just as the scout had promised.

Darkness now engulfed them on all sides as they drove deeper into the valley, allowing the wagons and animals in the rear to get clear of the canyon. Shouts sounded from ahead as the sentinels scouted for a clearing large enough for an encampment. Finally, the trumpet blew, sounding the end of a long, hard day of travel.

Paradine watched as Wills led the lead wagon in the usual wide arc. The others soon followed, forming the usual camp circle.

As his wife and son began to unload the wagon for the night, Paradine unhitched his oxen and led them a short distance from the camp, where they could graze. As he scanned the ground with his lantern, however, he became troubled.

"Doesn't look good, Willy. . . ."

Beneath his feet, the short grass was withered and brown. There was an unusual brittleness to it, lending a subtle crunch beneath his boots as he walked. Moving farther from the wagons, turning and throwing his light on one spot after another, he found the same predicament wherever he looked.

It's dead. . .all of it.

He noticed an object lying in the grass. Bending down, he picked up a soup spoon, tarnished almost black.

Well, someone else has *been here—*

He was troubled. A bad situation had just become much worse. They had to find a suitable grazing area, or else the oxen would go hungry, become weakened, and be unable to continue. Soon, they would die. And if the oxen perished, so would everyone else.

The surrounding area showed no signs of life at all, as if it were sterile. He knelt, running his hand through the lifeless blades, and quickly realized something else.

They were frozen.

But, this place isn't cold enough for—

Then, suddenly, it *was.*

Paradine felt a pressure against his eardrums as the still air became damp and frigid. In seconds, the temperature fell below freezing. Though he could not feel the gelid air moving, he nonetheless detected a motion, an ethereal sensation of currents coursing like those of an icy river, changing direction.

He sprang to his feet and whirled as a voice seemed to speak to him, a whisper softly echoing only inches from his ear. Just a few words, words he could not make out, in a language he did not know, in a voice that terrified him.

His heart pounded wildly. He broke out in a cold sweat. His hands and limbs trembled.

Never had he known such fear.

He dropped his lantern and on jelly legs broke into a dead run, leaving the oxen behind. Something huge and silent, he feared, was right behind him, giving chase. His intellect struggled against his instincts, fighting to remain in control.

Get hold of yourself! You didn't see *anything!*

Clearing the zone of unearthly cold, he rounded the periphery of the circled train and hurried toward the lead wagon. He found Wills standing still, staring up at the driver's seat, apprehension in his eyes.

"Captain," Paradine began, looking back over his shoulder, "we have a problem. There's something. . . "

He let the words trail off. Wills, his face grim, cut him a sideward glance.

"Yes," the wagon master whispered hoarsely. "We do."

Paradine reluctantly turned and followed Wills' gaze. There, right where he had been seated the entire day, Johnny sat slumped to one side, his eyes open, his features locked and unmoving.

The man was dead, and had been for some time.

"We need to get out of here," Paradine insisted. *"Something's* here. . .don't know what, and really don't care. There's nothing for the oxen. Ground's frozen. Grass is dead. . . "

"You don't have to convince me none." Wills nodded, signaling for Quonset. "Hair's been standing up on the back of my neck since we stopped. Whole place feels wrong."

The sentinel arrived, and Wills began to issue hurried orders.

"Get on your horse," he barked, more animated than usual. "Go back to the entry canyon and make sure this isn't some kind of trap. Report back as fast as you can. If you see *anything,* and by that I mean Indians or bandits or whatever, fire off a couple of warning rounds. And *hurry*. . .we're loading back up and getting out of here."

"Yes, sir," the man nodded, without question, running for his mount.

As the thunder of hoofbeats erupted and faded, Wills reached up, grabbed the body of the scout, and pulled it down. Paradine took the man by the boots, and they carried him clear of the wagons and into the darkness before lowering him to the hard ground.

"I'm sorry, Johnny," he said in a low voice. "Ain't got time for a burial. . . ."

The cold reached them, swirling around their legs, whitening their breath.

"Not a word of this, Mr. Paradine," Wills ordered. "No one's to know. . .not yet."

"You have my promise."

They returned to the camp. All seemed perfectly normal.

"Now what?" Paradine asked.

"We leave the way we came in. . .set up camp outside, at the base of the mountains, and wait for morning. Plenty of grass out there, and by daylight we can do some scouting and decide if this cutoff's such a good idea after all."

"I'm for that." Looking back in the direction of his oxen, he knew he had to round them up.

As Wills gave further orders to his men, Paradine broke away and returned to his wagon. Quietly grabbing a rifle from the long wooden box affixed to its side—he did not wish to alarm his family—he cautiously headed back toward his fallen lantern, toward the spot where he had left the oxen.

Nothing here, he reassured himself. *Nothing but the cold— nothing in the dark that isn't there in the light.*

Had it been a graveyard, he would have been whistling.

Upon arrival, he recovered the light and held it high, straining against the darkness.

His animals were gone.

"No, no, *no!*" he cried in frustration. "This is *not* the time to be wandering off!"

Searching frantically, he found a few random hoof prints, but no other sign of the beasts themselves. After several minutes, frightened to move any farther from camp, he decided he had wasted enough time and returned to his wagon. A measure of relief filled him as he paused to lean against its familiar sideboards.

"Lisabeth!" he called out, walking around front.

"Right here," she answered, leaning out from under the bonnet. "I know you didn't want buffalo again, but—"

"There's no time for that now. We're leaving here right away."

"At night?"

In frustration, he smacked a hand against the vacant yoke. "*If I can find our oxen.*"

"Daniel, what is it? Why are you carrying that rifle?"

"We have to get out of here. . . . "

"Indians?" she asked fearfully.

"No," he firmly replied. "Not Indians. But the captain wants to get back outside the pass and wait for daylight before we pass through here."

"When we're sitting still and settled in? He wants to leave, then come back? Daniel Paradine, you're not making a lick of sense."

"I know," he admitted. "But we'll discuss it later. Make sure everything's packed up, and in a hurry."

"It is. . .we barely got started *un*packing."

"Good. Where's Michael?"

"Here, Daddy," the boy piped up from behind his mother.

Relieved, Paradine turned again in the general direction of his missing livestock. "You two sit tight. . .I'm going to get some help and find Willy and the others."

Rifle still in hand, he ran back toward the lead wagon, noting along the way that the rest of the camp had gotten word to strike camp. All were resecuring the few items they had removed from their wagons, and muttering questions and complaints to each other.

"Captain," he began, upon reaching the man. "My oxen are missing. I need help in rounding them up."

The wagon master shook his head. "Mr. Paradine, take anyone you like who isn't otherwise tied up. But be quick about it. . . we're getting out of here as soon as I get the good word from Quonset."

"Thanks," Paradine said, turning to run. "I'll—"

"Captain Wills!" Another man ran up, all out of breath. "My mules. . .are gone. All ten just. . .disappeared."

"Not you, too," the leader began. "Mr. Paradine here—"

"I looked all around the camp, but—"

"Look, Arty," Wills cut in, shaking his head in frustration. "Can't you people keep up with your own animals? Why'd you unhitch 'em so quick, anyway?"

"I thought we were settled in. . .never had a problem with 'em wandering off before. I swear. . .I couldn't have turned my back for more than a minute."

"Well, apparently it was long enough."

"And I'm not the only one. Jeb Lassiter's missing all his oxen and both horses."

"All right," Wills said. "Get back to your wagon, and I'll send some men over as soon as I can spare 'em."

"Thank you, Captain." The man hurried away.

"Indians, you think?" Paradine asked.

"I doubt it," Wills said. "In my experience, they only steal horses, not draft animals. Anything's possible, I guess, but—"

He was interrupted by the pounding of hooves. Quonset pulled alongside, his lantern swinging on its saddle hook as his mount came to a stop.

"What do you think?" the wagon master asked, a tinge of hope in his voice.

"Gone," the man said, shaking his head.

"*What's* gone?" Wills winced. "Suddenly, we're losing everything we—"

"The canyon," Quonset said. "Ain't there no more. Nothing but sheer wall all the way across."

"That's impossible," Wills insisted. "You looked in the wrong place."

"No," the sentinel snapped. "I didn't. Followed the wheel marks all the way back. They just. . .*stopped*. . .right at the base of the rock."

"Could it have been a landslide?" Paradine offered.

"Did you *hear* a landslide?" the sentinel asked impatiently. "I'm tellin' you, Captain. . .it's like that pass was never there."

Wills closed his eyes.

"With this kind of dark," Quonset went on, "I don't know how we're getting out of here. But it *sure* ain't the same way we came in."

Chapter 3

The three men acted in secret, under the cover of darkness. They were as far from the others as they deemed safe, their deed clandestine to avoid causing a panic.

"Hardest ground I ever broke," said Garrett, patting the refilled grave with the back of his shovel.

"No marker?" Quonset asked.

"No marker," Wills said. "Don't want them to see. His Maker knows where he is. Good enough for Moses. . .good enough for Johnny."

He stared at the earthen mound, his head bowed, his mind a swirl of restless concerns. "But I think a moment here would be in order."

The three stood silently as they considered the grave, their hats in their hands, their thoughts the same—and less than reverent.

I hope you haven't dragged us all down there with you.

◉ ◉ ◉

No stars.

Paradine, cradling his rifle, peered upward from just inside his wagon. The quilt draped around his shoulders had done a fair job of keeping away the cold, except for his unprotected hands and face. Sleep had not come to him, though his wife and son, unaware of the gravity of their situation, had found rest. He turned and looked back to where they lay, asleep beneath their blankets on the floor of the wagon. There had been no tents that night, no sleeping outside—rather, much of their cargo had been removed and stacked on the ground, leaving room for them to spend the night in the relative safety of the Yankee bed.

He reached beneath the blanket and checked his pocket watch.

Almost four.

His fingers ached. It was so cold and so quiet—for the first time since their journey began, the night was silent. No droning of crickets, no howling of wolves, no whistle of wind. Even their own animals were strangely hushed, as if afraid to give themselves away to whatever lay in the darkness.

It had been an uneasy night, to say the least. Those still in the dark, so to speak, about their true situation were sleeping fitfully enough, but a few pairs of bleary eyes were still open. All had been told by the captain that a pack of particularly bold wolves was believed to be on the prowl, and that sleeping up inside the wagons was the prudent option for the night. Everyone had complied, assured that the sentinels would be patrolling the outer perimeter all night.

Paradine had tried to pass the hours by reading his first-edition copy of a novel entitled *A Christmas Carol*—signed by the author at a reading before a packed auditorium, during one of his American tours—but he found it difficult to concentrate.

Again, he forced his eyes to the page, that he might find a measure of escape, however momentary.

Darkness is cheap, he read, *and Scrooge liked it.*

"Well, sir," Paradine whispered to himself, "I have just the place for you...."

Sounds of stirring caught his ears. Looking across the way, he saw the sentinels once more walking from wagon to wagon, waking those who slept. For most, it would seem like an ordinary morning, following the ordinary routine with no expectation but that of another long day on the trail.

If only, he wished.

◉ ◉ ◉

Jeb Lassiter nudged his friend in the adjoining wagon, waking him from a sound sleep.

"What?" Arty Sutton asked, half-aware, his reddened eyes searching. "What is it?"

His gaze fell upon the face hovering close above him. The two upper front teeth capped in gold, which shone even in the meager light, revealed the man's identity.

"Jeb," Sutton said wearily, "what do you want? I'm beat...go get some sleep."

"Shhhh," Lassiter whispered, careful not to rouse the man's

wife and family. "Come on, Arty. . .we're goin' out to find our livestock."

"Now?" Sutton asked, rubbing his head. "What time is it?"

"About a hour to sunup. We'll be back before anyone knows we're missing."

"Why don't we just wait? Captain said—"

"The longer we wait, the farther they're gonna wander off. And if we wait on Wills, he's not gonna give us time to search."

"Go ask him."

"You know there's no way he's gonna let us wander off, not after what happened at Chimney Rock."

Sutton thought back, recalling the wagon master's anger the time a man and his sons, late returning from their search for a fishing hole, had held up the wagons for more than an hour.

"Yeah," he assented, gently rising from his bed. "Okay."

◉ ◉ ◉

"Daniel, you've barely touched your breakfast."

Paradine did not hear her.

"Daniel. . . ?" Lisabeth repeated, more loudly.

"Oh, I'm sorry. . .I was just thinking about the oxen."

"As soon as it gets light, you'll find them easily enough. Stop worrying. . .you'll need your strength for the day. Eat."

He took another bite of his scrambled eggs, watching as his wife and son also partook of their meals. His mind was a sea of worry, a torrent of doubt.

He checked his watch.

"You're probably right," he said. "Should be getting light soon."

"By six-thirty, for sure," Michael said. "Even with the mountains."

"Yes," his father confirmed. "Same as always."

Paradine scanned the starless sky above, longing for some sign of the coming sunrise. A wisp of purple, a scattering of orange.

He found only the same starless black he had seen all night.

He checked his watch again.

Setting his tin plate on a wooden box, he took a last swallow of coffee, calmly rose to his feet, and stretched. "I'm going to see the captain. I'll be right back."

"All right, darling," Lisabeth said. "Don't be long. I'll need help getting all these things back into the wagon."

He looked at the trunks and items of furniture to which she referred and found himself thinking of them only in terms of their weight.

"We may want to leave a few of those things here," he said, to the surprise of his wife. "But we'll discuss that when I get back."

He realized his mind-set had changed—no longer was their journey a quest. Now, it had become an *escape,* and anything that might slow their flight, in his eyes, carried a new lethality.

Paradine took up his rifle and a lantern and cut across the camp. As he neared the lead wagon, he found no sign of Wills.

"Captain?" he called. No response.

He walked around to the other side and found the man kneeling in the brown grass, his back softly illuminated by a hanging lantern. Paradine stopped at the rear corner of the wagon and waited, not wanting to interrupt. In a moment, the prayer ended, and the man rose to his feet.

"Captain?" the teacher repeated softly as he approached the leader, who stood looking upward.

"Mr. Paradine."

"What time do you have?"

"Same as you."

Paradine pulled his watch from his pocket and opened it. "Are you sure?"

"I'm sure."

After a lengthy pause, the teacher spoke again. "What are we going to do?"

"That, I don't know," said the wagon master.

"You're going to have to tell them *something*."

"I'm open to suggestions, Mr. Paradine," he said grimly. "Just how do you tell a group of people that you led them into hell?"

Paradine stood silently watching Wills, who continued to gaze upward, unmoving.

"They're going to know any minute," Paradine said. "I'm surprised they don't already."

No reply.

Paradine checked his watch again.

Seven forty-three.

◉ ◉ ◉

Inside their wagon, Michael reached into the wooden box filled with important papers, photographs, and other personal items. With both hands he carefully withdrew the family Bible.

"Maybe we could read a little more. . .just until Daddy gets back," he said, holding the Bible out toward his mother.

She smiled and took the book from him, then opened it as he snuggled up against her. "What shall we read, then?" she asked the boy, testing him. "Where were we?"

"The book of Mark," he answered.

"That's right," she said, kissing him on the forehead. "Let's see, now. . . "

"Right there," he pointed, indicating a verse.

Lisabeth began to read.

"And they came over unto the other side of the sea, into the country of the Gadarenes. And when He was come out of the ship, immediately there met him out of the tombs a man with an unclean spirit, who had his dwelling among the tombs; and no man could bind him, no, not with chains, because that he had been often bound with fetters and chains, and the chains had been plucked asunder by him, and the fetters broken in pieces; neither could any man tame him.

"And always, night and day, he was in the mountains, and in the tombs, crying and cutting himself with stones. But when he saw Jesus afar off, he ran and worshipped him, and cried with a loud voice, and said, What have I to do with thee, Jesus, thou Son of the most high God? I adjure thee by God, that thou torment me not.

"For He said unto him, Come out of the man, thou unclean spirit. And He asked him, What is thy name?

"And he answered, saying, My name is Legion, for we are many. And he besought him much that he would not send them away out of the country.

"Now there was there nigh unto the mountains a great herd of swine feeding. And all the devils besought him, saying, Send us into the swine, that we may enter into them. And forthwith Jesus gave them leave. And the unclean spirits went out, and entered into the swine. And the herd ran violently down a steep place into the sea, (they were about two thousand;) and were choked in the sea. And they that fed the swine fled, and told it in the city, and in the country."

"What does that mean, Mama?" the boy asked.

"Well," the woman replied, "there were a lot of demons inside that man. . .two thousand of them. And Jesus made them leave him, and sent them into a great big herd of pigs. . .and the animals went mad and drowned themselves in the sea."

"But why would they want to be inside of pigs?"

"I guess it was either that or wander the earth without any form at all, because Jesus wasn't about to let them into any other people."

"Oh."

The woman tried to continue the reading, but she was interrupted by voices from the adjoining wagon.

Loud voices. Panicked voices.

She set the book down as she began to catch a few of their words.

"Stay right here, Michael," she said, rising. "I'll be right back. You can go ahead and put the Bible away for now."

"Yes, ma'am."

Lisabeth lowered herself from the rear of the wagon, walked around front, and approached the neighboring family. A man was speaking to his wife. Lisabeth caught only a few words.

". . .no matter what George says. It just can't be. . ."

"What is it?" Lisabeth asked, seeing the fear on their faces. "What's wrong?"

"I'll tell you what's wrong," the woman said. "Anna Russell just told me it's almost eight o'clock."

"That can't be," Lisabeth said. "It's still dark."

"That's what I said. But she said the captain's watch said the same thing, and so did Mr. Perryman's."

Lisabeth spun toward the lead wagon. In the distance, she saw the dim glow of a moving lantern, drawing closer.

Daniel!

◎ ◎ ◎

As Paradine approached, his boots crunching on the frozen grass, Lisabeth ran to him, closing the final distance.

"Eliza May just told me that it's almost eight—"

"Come on," he insisted, taking her by the arm, leading her back toward their wagon.

"But what she said—"

"What she said," he whispered, then paused for a drawn-out moment, "is *true.*"

Lisabeth's face became a mask of confusion. He tried to hurry her along but was stopped by insistent words from behind.

"Paradine!" shouted Eliza May's husband, Ben Taylor. "You got a watch. . .what's it say?"

The teacher stopped and turned.

"It says we're in trouble," he announced flatly, knowing that no longer was there any point in trying to hide the truth. "And any minute now, the captain's going to—"

"It's the end of the world!" Eliza May cried, trembling. "The Day of Judgment, great and terrible to—"

"It's *not* the end of the world," Paradine said firmly. "I know that much."

"How can you be so sure?" Taylor demanded, holding his frantic wife.

"I just *know*. . .I promise you, the universe doesn't work that way."

A woman's scream pierced the darkness.

Chapter 4

Wills turned sharply at the sound.
It was no mere scream—it was the cry of a banshee, a shriek of unbridled terror.

Adrenaline flooded his veins, driving his heart up into his throat. Instinctively, his fingers lanced out and found the barrel of his rifle, tearing it from its resting place against a wagon wheel. In one motion, he whirled with the weapon, took up his lantern, and broke into a dead run in the direction of the cry.

◉ ◉ ◉

Every man sprang into action, grabbing his weapons and trailing after the wagon master. Some took up rifles; others brandished pistols, knives, shovels, and axes. Across the camp they headed, disappearing into the smothering darkness, their lanterns barely visible as they reached the edge of the camp.

As Paradine took a first hurried step, he found his arm caught. Jarred to a stop, he turned to find Lisabeth desperately clutching his wrist.

"No," she implored him, fear glinting in her wet eyes. "Let the others handle it. Please, Daniel—"

◎ ◎ ◎

Wills, tracing the circle of the camp, was the first to arrive at the scene. Initially, he saw no one, his eyes darting in a frantic search, scanning the trio of darkened wagons facing away from him just ahead. Two were dark, but the center wagon was dimly lit by the faint glow of a lamp hanging against its side.

The forward section of the first wagon was smashed, its yokes and animals missing altogether. Wills saw no sign of the wagon's owners, who only moments before had been packing their belongings, preparing to leave.

Inching forward toward the second wagon, he heard muffled sobs from within. Slowly lifting the flap, he peered inside. At the far end, her face buried in her hands, a woman wept hysterically.

"Marjorie," Wills called softly, placing a hand atop the rear boards.

She jumped at the sound and whirled, a fresh scream erupting from her lips.

"It's all right," he said, trying to calm her. "It's only me. . . Jeremiah. . . "

"*Sam,*" she managed to say, her voice breaking. "He's—"

"Where is he?" Wills asked. He knew her husband well.

"He's—He's—" Her words muddled by sobs, she turned and looked down from the open front. "He's. . .*there*. . . "

"I'm coming around," Wills said gently.

He eased away from the rear of the wagon and crept along the side, his rifle cocked and at the ready. Ahead, a candle lamp squeaked on its bracket as it swung in the cool breeze, casting faint, moving shadows at the front of the wagon. He drew near, his every step punctuated by the sounds of the woman's uncontrolled grief.

Rifle raised, he came around the front.

The wagon's yoke tongue had been splintered. The oxen were nowhere to be seen. Blood heavily splattered the front of the bonnet, the wagon, the ground.

Lying beneath the broken hitch, face up, was what was left of Samuel Carter.

Wills came to a halt a few feet from the body. As he stared in disbelief, fighting the bile rising in his throat, frenzied footsteps thundered up behind him. On edge, he whirled to find a dozen men at his back, their arms at the ready.

"Hold up!" the wagon master shouted, an arm out to stop them.

The men came to a sudden halt, some slipping a bit on the frozen ground. They stared past each other, silenced by their horror, struggling to comprehend the scene.

"You men," Wills ordered, "get back to your wagons, right now. You, Gordon and Asa. . .you stay here."

The men paused, their weapons still raised.

"*Now!*" Wills repeated, more forcefully. "Looks like we're dealing with grizzlies, most likely. . .and I don't like the idea of your families sitting there alone without you."

Without another word, the men turned and hurried back toward the main camp. Garrett and Quonset approached, surveyed the damage, and looked to Wills with questions in their eyes.

"Grizzlies?" Garrett asked.

Wills gave no further reply. He reached up into the wagon, pulled free a linen bedsheet, and draped it over the body. Blood immediately seeped through, emphasizing the number and severity of the wounds.

"Captain," Garrett went on, his tone doubtful, "I've seen a lot of bear attacks in my day, and when they—"

"Now's not the time, Asa."

"But. . ."

"I said, *later.*"

Wills leaned into the open front of the wagon and spoke gently to the grieving widow. "Marjorie. . .what happened? What did you see?"

The woman continued to wail.

"Please," he tried again. "We have to know."

Marjorie tried to gather herself. She took several shaky breaths, determined to be brave.

"I was. . .I was in the back of the wagon. . ."

All eyes were on her.

"Just. . .packing up. . .like always. . ." She paused, as if struggling to remember, as if the event had occurred years before.

"And?" Wills gently pressed. "Marjorie, what happened then?"

She looked into his eyes. "And then, the wagon. . .*shook*. . .a terrible. . ."

"A terrible. . .*what*. . . ?"

"A sound. . .but nothing like. . .and it shook again. . .and I

64

crawled to the front of the wagon, and looked out. . .and the oxen were just. . .*gone.*" A sob began to rise in her throat. "And. . .and Sam was. . ."

She went silent. Not wishing to push any further, Wills let her be.

"That's fine, Marjorie," he said. "You done good."

The wagon master turned to Garrett.

"Get her to the other side of the camp," he said quietly. "Make sure someone there stays with her. . .I don't want her left alone for a second."

"Yes, sir," the man said.

"And keep a sharp eye. Cut straight across the camp, and keep that lantern high and your rifle ready. Move quick. . .we'll be right behind you."

Quonset stepped forward and helped Garrett as he lifted the woman, who was clearly in shock, out of the wagon.

"Won't matter," Marjorie said with cold detachment, as her feet came to rest on the bloodied ground. "We're not getting out of here alive. We're going to die. . .all of us."

The men said nothing in response as Garrett led the woman gingerly away, leaving only Wills and his second-in-command at the scene.

"Bless her," Wills said, shaking his head. "They'd only been married a year."

The silence pressed in upon them.

"*Grizzlies,* Captain?" Quonset asked, lifting the red-stained sheet from the body enough to afford a view of the carnage beneath. "You really think *bears* did *this?*" He dropped the linen. "The man's torn apart. . .and from what the wife said, it happened in seconds, if that. And this yoke. . .it's solid oak, but look at it. That kind of damage would take a force of—"

"*Of course* it weren't bears," Wills said, his voice low, his tone grave.

"Then, *what?*" Quonset asked.

"Come here."

Wills took the lantern and led the way to the front of the next wagon, about twenty-five feet away.

It was fractured and broken up in several places, as Wills knew it would be. The livestock, the occupants—all were gone.

"You used to fix wagons for a living, didn't you?" the captain asked.

"For years," Quonset answered. "Whole time I was in Kentucky."

"You ever seen anything like this?"

"No," the man said. "Wood looks *twisted*. . .bent every which way."

"It's the same with the next wagon back," Wills said. "All three, splintered up like a tornado come through. What kind of animal could do that? Nothing *I* ever heard of." He looked at the wreckage. "The Thomsons and the Lindseys were good people. And poor Sam. . ."

"Heaven help us," Quonset whispered.

"I've spent the better part of thirty years out here," Wills said. "First with the cavalry, and then. . . " His voice trailed away as a thousand memories flashed through his mind. "I figured I'd seen just about anything a man could see, west of the Mississippi. . . but I don't have a clue what could have done this. Whatever it was, it smashed these wagons like nothin', and it carried off almost a dozen people, including women and children, and twice that many oxen."

"So why'd it spare Marjorie?"

"Don't know. It. . .or *they*. . .who knows how many there are?

Maybe it just didn't see her."

"S'pose they're all dead? The folks, I mean."

"Don't know that either."

"No other bodies. . .no blood. . .*might* be a good sign."

"Maybe. Here. . .help me. We'll need these." Moving from wagon to wagon, the two pulled the unlit lanterns from their hooks.

When the wagon master had come around again near the shrouded body, he held his light high.

"Weird. . .the light don't carry more'n a few feet. Like the dark was. . ." The word escaped him. "Like it's—"

"*Thicker* than usual," Quonset finished. "No fog or nothing, but the light just falls away. Never seen such a thing."

"Look at that," Wills said, examining the damaged yoke once again. "At the rate we're losing draft animals, we're *never* getting out of here. Paradine and Sutton already couldn't find theirs, and now. . ." He groaned in frustration. "That's *half* our wagons, with nothing left to pull 'em."

"Maybe if we abandon those, or split up the teams we still have—"

"Splitting the teams won't help. Two or three oxen can't pull a wagon any distance. We'll *have* to leave the damaged ones, if their yokes are ruined. All the oxen in the world won't help you if you don't have a way to hitch 'em up."

"I know, boss, but—"

"I just hope we don't lose any more."

"What if we *do?*"

Wills shook his head, hating the thought of what he was about to say. "Then we're going to have to go *find* 'em. Likely have to do that anyway."

"In *this* dark? Think they're even alive?"

"They'd better be."

"And if they're not?"

"We'll cross that river when we get there."

"Jeremiah," Quonset said grimly, "I think we're there *already.*"

They examined the area around the body more closely, following the pattern of blood on the ground until it gradually gave out about thirty feet beyond the farthest wagon.

"Look at that. . .the grass. . . "

Quonset caught on. "How can that be?"

"Not one hoof print or drag mark leading away. Just the blood—and not too much of that either. How in the world can you—"

Wills fell silent as a new sound began to rise in the darkness. He sensed a change in the air pressure.

"Do you hear that?" Quonset whispered. "Kind of a big. . . *breathing. . .*"

"Smell that?" Wills dared, as a sulfurous stench wafted into his nostrils.

Looking up, they sensed more than saw a motion, deeper into the viscous black. Startled, both men froze, their hearts pounding. Their eyes strained against the void for something they dreaded to see, searching from side to side as they rose to their feet.

Falling back a few steps, they fired into the pitch darkness, again and again. There was no sign of impact, no bellows of pain. Their bullets found no target.

Spinning away, dragging their expended rifles and their lanterns, the men raced as fast as their legs would carry them toward the others, toward what they now knew was pure fiction: safety in numbers.

◎ ◎ ◎

Lisabeth and a couple of the other women helped Marjorie into a wagon, where she was laid upon a bed, still shaking.

"Eliza May gave her laudanum," Lisabeth said, standing at its rear. "Hopefully, she'll be able to rest."

"Bless her heart," said Paradine, handing up a quilt he had brought from their wagon.

"To lose Sam that way, and right in front of her. . ."

She fell silent and stepped away, lowering her eyes. Paradine knew from the look on her face that she was playing the scene over in her mind—with herself as the new widow.

"Now listen," he said calmly and firmly. "Nothing's going to happen to me, or to you, or to Michael. We're going to be fine. We know what we're up against now. Poor Sam wasn't looking to be attacked, and he wasn't ready. I doubt he even had a rifle loaded."

"*You* did," she said.

"What?"

"All night. . .you had a rifle ready. Why?"

"I didn't know where the oxen had gone, and—"

"Don't lie to me, Daniel Paradine. You knew something was out there, didn't you? That's why you had us sleep in the wagon. Why didn't you tell everyone? Why didn't you tell *Sam?*"

He averted his eyes.

"I didn't. . .*know,*" he told her. "I knew *something* was going on. Seemed like it, anyway. Something weird. I talked to the captain about it. . .turned out I wasn't the only one missing livestock. But he didn't want to stir a panic without good cause."

"Good cause?" she asked. "Well, I guess we have good cause *now,* don't we?"

"Lisabeth," he implored her, "if he'd alerted the whole camp, and *everyone* got the jitters like I had last night, could have been some shots fired at oxen, or horses, or worse. Folks' imaginations tend to go wild in the dark. . .they see things that aren't there. Mistake one thing for another, and—" He stopped, his own mind filled with doubts.

"I know," she said, placing a loving hand against his cheek. "It was the captain's decision to make. He's in charge. We knew that when we signed on for this trip. I guess things are always so much clearer in hindsight. . . ."

Paradine leaned against the wagon and rubbed his eyes.

"I am *so* tired. . . "

"Didn't you sleep at all?"

"Not a bit. I may have dozed for a few seconds, here and there. I'm not sure."

"Why don't you lie down," Lisabeth offered, leading him toward their wagon. "Try to get a *little* rest, anyway. We'll wake you if anything happens."

◎ ◎ ◎

Lassiter, his feet aching in the cold, held his lantern out in front of himself, but the bright red light failed to pierce the darkness.

Come on, he worried, seeing no sign of his livestock. *Where did you go?*

"I don't get it," Sutton said, holding the collar of his heavy coat closed with one hand. "It has to be after seven by now. We've been gone for hours."

"Lucky break," the man replied. "Must've been earlier than I thought."

"Never known it to be so still. . .or so quiet. I mean, listen. There's nothing."

"This ain't the prairie. Things are different in the mountains."

"I didn't want to be out here this long. We're missin' too much sleep, and we're gonna need it tomorrow. . .I mean, today. . . "

"How could they have wandered off so far?" Lassiter groaned. "I bet we've covered half a mile."

"Probably been going in circles. Wish I knew what was wrong with that stupid compass of yours. . . ."

"Maybe there's iron ore in these mountains. Lodestone even. How should I know?"

"Got us good and lost."

"Quit worrying. . .I'll get us back."

Lassiter turned to his left, bringing the light around. Up ahead, he could make out the faint outline of something sizable.

"There," he said, starting forward. In moments, they were close enough to recognize the shape in the murky darkness.

"It's just another wagon," Sutton said in frustration. "How many of these are we gonna find? What's this make, a dozen or more? All broken down, all stripped of supplies."

Lassiter held his light inside it, finding only bare wood for his trouble. "Indians," he muttered. "H. . .had to be. These folks came into this valley, same as we did, and got attacked. Must've happened years ago, though. . .these wagons *all* look old. Cloth's rotted. . .wood's dried out. . .they're in bad shape."

"Axles broken, yokes chopped to pieces. Thing's almost on its side."

"Kinda looks like it *fell* there or something," Lassiter noted, "the way it's laying."

"What if they're still here?" Sutton said. "The Indians, I mean. What if our animals didn't just wander off? What if they got stolen? What if they're getting ready to attack at any time, and—"

"What if, what if," Lassiter interrupted. "Indians don't care nothin' about oxen."

"Maybe they just want to strand us, so we can't get away."

Lassiter mulled that over for a moment. "Could be, I guess."

"We better get back, Jeb. It just don't feel right out here. . .not one bit. And it's a lot colder'n it was just a few minutes ago."

"All right," the other man agreed stubbornly. "We'll try again after daybreak. . .if Wills lets us, that is."

"So," Sutton began, with forced calmness, "which way to camp?"

Lassiter paused, looking around, his face bathed in the harsh lamplight, his front teeth glinting gold.

"That way," he said firmly.

"You sure?"

"Yes, I'm sure."

"How do you know?"

"I just do."

They had taken no more than a few steps when something else caught their eye, well off to one side.

"Look there," Lassiter indicated. "That ain't a wagon."

They moved closer. Whatever it was began to sparkle in the light from the lantern.

Gold? Lassiter wondered. *No—ain't yellow enough—*

Then they were upon it.

"Waterhole," Sutton said. "But, it's frozen. All the way through, from the look of it."

"It was nearly a hundred degrees today. How could it have frozen so fast? Didn't get *that* cold tonight."

"I don't know, but I don't like it."

They walked around the edge of the frozen pool, moving in

the general direction of the camp, according to Lassiter.

As they reached the far side, something else appeared in the inky blackness—a horse, on its knees at the edge of the frozen pond, its muzzle against the ice.

"Oh, no," Lassiter said, coming to a stop. "I think it's dead."

"One of yours?" Sutton asked, lagging a few steps behind.

"No," he said in horror. "I think it died a long time ago."

Sutton caught up and stood beside his friend. "Look at that. . ."

The horse's mouth and nose were embedded in the ice. A white frost covered its once-black coat.

"Looks like it died in mid-swallow," Sutton said. "Like the water just suddenly froze up." He shook his head in amazement. "Now how can that be?"

"Gets worse," Lassiter said, moving fully around to the other side of the carcass. *"Lots* worse."

Most of the animal's belly and midsection were missing, as if they'd been devoured by some immense, savage beast. Frost covered its ribcage, left exposed by the absence of internal organs.

"Wolves didn't do *that,"* Lassiter said. "Something. . .*bigger.*"

"I really, *really* don't like it out here," Sutton said, unable to tear his eyes from the grisly sight.

Fearful now of predators, they broke into a dead run, their rifles cocked and ready. Neither man said a word as they ran, their heavy, gulping breaths fogging briefly in the chill air before quickly trailing behind.

The temperature continued to plunge. A wind rose out of nowhere, blasting the two men with walls of icy air. Knocked from their feet, they struggled to rise again, only to be tossed anew by the roaring, brutal force.

A glitter of frost began to form on their clothing, growing

thicker and whiter each second. Their lanterns dimmed.

Something suddenly towered over them. Something huge.

Fumbling with frostbitten fingers against the storm, they fired their rifles. The thing began to lean down, its glistening, yellow eyes catching the final remnant of the lanterns' fading glow.

Then, the light was gone.

Lassiter heard a tearing of fabric and flesh from the place where Sutton lay.

No one heard their screams.

Wills and Quonset emerged from the darkness, laden with recovered lanterns, dragging their guns. The light of the still-burning breakfast fires beckoned them back to the circle of wagons.

"Ladies and gentlemen," the captain announced, out of breath, lowering his load to the ground as all eyes turned, "we need to talk."

A crowd quickly gathered, wrapped in coats and blankets against the cold. Paradine rose from his bed and climbed down out of the wagon.

"What is all this?" one man demanded. "What's happening?"

"I'm sure you all heard the rifle shots," Wills began, his frosty breath visible.

Puzzled faces answered him, and several shook their heads *no*.

"How could you *not* have?" Quonset wondered, astonished. "We were just over there. . .barely a hundred feet away."

"No matter," Wills went on. "We saw and heard something moving around out there, in the dark, beyond the wagons. Something big. . .like a grizzly raised up on its hind legs, or—"

He chose to stop there. "Anyway, we took a few shots. . .don't know if we hit it or not."

The congregation fearfully scanned the darkness around them.

"The problem is this," Wills continued. "We're missing live-stock, now. . .oxen, mules—"

"And horses," Forrester called out. "I just checked. Four of the saddled mounts are gone, along with seven others. That leaves us with five, and only three saddles that I know of."

"And *men,*" shouted Garrett.

"What?" Wills asked.

The grizzled man stepped forward. "Just took a head count. Jeb Lassiter and Arty Sutton are missing."

Wills momentarily closed his eyes, wincing at the bad news.

"He went after his livestock," Billy Lassiter, Jeb's young son, said. "I wasn't supposed to tell, but I saw him as he was leaving. He took his railroad lamp—the one with the red glass in it. I wanted to go, but he wouldn't let me. Said he'd be back in an hour. But that was a long time ago."

Wills looked into the face of Lassiter's wife, who stood next to her son.

"I'm sorry, Ma," the boy said to her. "He made me promise."

She looked to the wagon master, her expression desperate.

"All right, people," Wills said, drawing a deep breath, "let's not panic. I'm sure they're just fine—out looking for their livestock. But *no one else leaves*. You got that? Not without my permission."

Quonset took over. "Okay, listen up. First priority for all of you, beyond your own safety and that of your families—do *not* let your livestock out of your sight. Pull them all into the cen-ter of the camp. Stand guard—*armed* guard. We can't afford to lose *one* more. Likely the ones we're missing just got spooked and are wandering around out there. They'd have sensed the bears early on."

Unspoken doubts registered on a few faces around the circle.

"Now. . .as you're well aware," Quonset glanced at his pocket watch, "it's almost a quarter after eight. If the sun had any intention of rising around here, it would've done it by now. I don't understand what's happening up there, and I'm not gonna pretend to, but it's still dark, and likely's gonna stay that way. That makes our job a lot harder, but we have no choice."

"What job?" Russell impatiently asked.

"First, finding Jeb and Arty. Second, bringing in our livestock. Third, finding another way out of here."

"What's wrong with the way we came in?" asked a woman.

"The way we came in ain't there no more," Quonset said frankly. "Looks like some kind of landslide or somethin' sealed off the pass. We were told the valley narrows into another passage on the other side, so we're going to have to try to scout it in the dark. But the first priority's getting those men and those lost animals back here."

"Where is he?" asked another. "This is all *his* fault."

"Who?" Wills stalled, knowing full well who was intended.

"Johnny—where's Johnny? He's the one who led us in here. Where is that little weasel?"

Wills looked to Quonset, who nodded assent.

"Dead," the wagon master blurted. "Died as soon as we got here. So, if you're lookin' to blame anyone, I reckon it'll have to be me."

A murmur swept the group.

"If you want to replace me, that's your right," Wills said. "But whatever you're gonna do, do it fast."

"We trust you, Captain," said a slight man named John

Forrester. "What's your call?"

Wills scanned the group. "Is that right? Does Forrester here speak for y'all? Do you trust me to lead us out of here?"

They nodded in agreement and a few voiced their assent. For now, anyway, he still had their confidence.

"All right then," Quonset said. "We'll need a few volunteers. We're gonna go out there and bring back our friends—and what's ours."

Paradine took up his rifle and stepped forward. "I'll help, Captain."

Lisabeth pulled gently at his arm, clearly unhappy about his decision.

"No thanks, bookworm," Garrett replied, cocking his percussion-lock shotgun. "We don't need the likes of you getting in the way out there. You stay put."

"That's enough, Asa," an angry Wills said. "It's not your decision. The last time I checked, *I* was the one leading this wagon train."

"And look where it got us," Garrett snapped.

"That'll do," Quonset barked, wrapping a huge, intimidating hand around the barrel of Garrett's rifle. "The captain'll get us all out of here, but only if we keep a cool head and don't panic."

"Won't be easy, once you get away from the camp," Forrester said, looking down at his pocket compass. "Thing can't find north."

Quonset looked over Forrester's shoulder. The needle was moving erratically and constantly. He checked his own.

"All right, so the compasses are out," he groaned. "We'll think of something else."

"Mr. Paradine," Wills said, shuffling his feet and fingering his rifle nervously, "maybe with all your book knowledge you have some ideas about what's causing this darkness. I'd appreciate it if you'd come along."

"I'd be honored."

The captain looked over the crowd. "Who else?"

◎ ◎ ◎

"Daniel Paradine," Lisabeth whispered to him, "you come back to me."

"I will," he said. "I promise." He looked toward their wagon, where Michael sat clutching the family Bible, fear showing on his soft, young face.

Paradine crossed the twenty or so feet between them and took a deep breath to steady his voice.

"I'm going to go help the others to find our animals," he said. "There will be plenty of men on guard here, to make sure you and your mother are safe until I get back."

"This is the valley in the Bible," Michael said, "isn't it?"

"What?" Paradine asked, caught off guard. "What valley?"

"The valley of the shadowy death," he said.

"That's shadow *of* death."

"We're in it, though. . .aren't we?"

"No," Paradine said, not altogether sure. "I don't think so."

"Well, if this *was* it," Michael said, "then God is here with us, and we aren't supposed to be afraid."

"I know."

"His rod and His staff are supposed to comfort us."

"I know."

"But. . .I *am* afraid, Daddy."

"Don't be. . .everything will be just fine."

The boy lowered his eyes. "It's all my fault."

"What is? What's your fault?"

"That we're here in the first place. If I hadn't wanted to come so badly—"

Paradine leaned his rifle against the wagon wheel, reached up, and took his son into his arms.

"Listen," he said. "Your mother and I were happy you were so excited about the trip, but we'd have come anyway. This opportunity is one I've hoped for a long, long time. Besides. . . ," he stroked the boy's hair, "hundreds of years from now, people will look at Independence Rock and see the name Michael Paradine engraved there. . .and they'll know that a fine young man once passed that way, a young man who always made his father very, very proud."

Michael recalled the sunny day, weeks before, when he had used a knife to cut his name and the date into the stone.

"That alone was worth the trip." His father smiled. "Don't you think?"

Seeing the continued fear in the boy's eyes, he resorted to words he did not fully believe. "God *is* here with you, and He'll see to it that you and your mother and I get through this valley safely."

"You're sure He is?"

"Yes, son," the man lied. "We're all going to make it to Saraleah, just like I said. I don't want you to be afraid. . .I'm sure there's a simple explanation for this long nighttime. We'll find out what it is."

The boy reached up and playfully tapped the lenses of his father's spectacles with a fingernail, as he often did. "Can I come with you to find Mr. Lassiter?"

"No, no," Paradine said softly. "I don't think your mother would be too happy about that. Besides, you need to stay here and be the man of the family until I get back."

"Okay, Daddy. . .I will."

A voice called out from the other side of the camp. "Hey, schoolteacher! You comin,' or ain't ya?"

Paradine hugged and kissed his son, then lowered him to the ground, turned, and picked up his rifle.

"I won't be long, Michael."

"Okay, Daddy. I love you."

"I love you, too, son."

◎ ◎ ◎

Paradine walked up to his wife, who had overheard the latter part of the conversation.

"Did you mean that?" she asked. "What you told him about God?"

"I'll be back in less than an hour," he pledged.

Despite her repeated prayers, despite her devotion, she knew his heart still was as dark as the valley around them.

Reaching out and up, she held him. She felt his jawline, covered with a day's stubble.

"You didn't have a shave this morning. I don't remember you ever missing one before."

"Something came up. Too bad it wasn't the sun."

They kissed tenderly, knowing it might be the last time.

"I love you," he whispered into her ear, their cheeks pressed together.

"You come back to me, Daniel Paradine."

Behind his glasses, his eyes were wet.

She pulled back, her arms still around him.

"God *does* love you," she said, as she had so many times

before. "You're not here by accident. None of us are. He saves His own. Whatever happens. . .it was meant to be."

"I'll try to remember that."

He took up a lantern, adjusted the flame, and disappeared into the darkness.

Chapter 5

"You know," the man said, his voice low, "I had an uncle who died at the Alamo."

"Did you really, John?" Paradine asked, knowing nothing about Forrester but his name.

"Yup. . .and after that, I swore I'd never volunteer for nothin'. Now look at me."

"Alamo looks real good right about now, huh?"

"No kidding," the sandy blond man agreed. "At least they knew what they were up against."

Lanterns held high and hearts pounding, the seven men ventured ever deeper into the darkness, all eyes and ears wide open, seeking any sign of their missing compatriots and their livestock.

Chayalocha

Again and again, as loudly as seemed safe, they called the men's names.

No reply came.

The party moved as one, a small island of dim, golden light in a vast sea of cold, velvet black, pressing forward slowly and deliberately. As a precaution against getting lost, the man bringing up the rear steadily unwound a ball of sturdy twine, tied at the other end to a wheel of one of the camp's wagons.

"How's the string holdin' out?" Wills asked.

"About half gone," the man replied. "Tied four spools together. . .figure we had about three hundred feet when we started."

"Okay," the leader said. "When we hit the end of it, we wind it back up and swing side-to-side until it brings us back to camp."

"Pretty smart," Garrett said.

"Only if we don't have to go more than three hundred feet," Wills said, acknowledging the flaw in his plan. "I don't want to go any farther than that, not at first. Main problem is, we have no way of knowing which way or how far Jeb and Arty went. A lot of prayer's in order, fellas."

Onward into the nothingness they drove, fearing for their friends—and for themselves.

"I can't get used to this," an uneasy Forrester said. "No crickets, no creek frogs, no night birds. . .nothing. Dead quiet. Ever since we entered the valley—"

"No smells in the air, either," Paradine noticed. "It's as if the place is. . .sterile."

"How can you have a place where nothing lives?" Garrett asked.

"*Something* lives here," Wills reminded them. "Sam Carter met it personal."

No one spoke after that, not for a while.

84

A short time later, their lights fell upon a familiar object.

Quonset knelt beside a broken yoke, fingering the splintered wood. "Useless. Split clear in two, lengthwise."

"How'd it get all the way out *here?*" Forrester wondered, looking back over his shoulder as if he could have seen the camp in the distance. "Could an ox have drug it this far?"

"*Something* did," Wills said.

"I'll tell you one thing," Quonset muttered, rising to his feet. "Landmarks sure would help. Nothing but dead grass. . .no rocks, no trees, no bushes. . ."

They continued on, their pace slow, deliberate, intense.

"Captain!" the man with the twine said suddenly, his voice rising as loud as he dared.

"What is it?"

"Something just. . .*tugged* on the string."

They all froze.

Okay, what does that mean? Paradine felt a sense of dread begin to stir in the pit of his stomach.

"You sure it didn't just hang on something?" Wills asked, walking back to him.

"Sure felt like a tug. . .but I guess *maybe* it could've gotten caught." He played it back and forth a bit. "Seems okay now. But, I'll tell you, Captain. . .if this had been a fishing line and if I'd been on the shore of a lake, I'd've landed a big one for sure by now. It was that kind of tug."

"Jeb, maybe?" Quonset wondered. "Or Arty?"

Wills pulled on the twine, which stretched back into the darkness behind them.

"Just keep playing it out," he said. "If it *was* them, they'll be smart enough to follow it one way or the other. . .either to us, or to the camp."

Twenty or thirty more feet fell behind them—then fifty. Still no landmarks.

"Can't be this way all the way out, can it?" Paradine wondered. "I mean, surely we'll hit *something.*"

"Mr. Paradine," Wills said, slowing to a stop, "you may have just gotten your wish."

The wagon master held his lamp higher and took a few more steps. Something rose before them at the edge of the lantern's throw, something huge, ghostly, and white.

"What *is* that?" whispered Garrett.

Wills drew steadily closer, his rifle up, his finger trembling on the trigger.

Another few steps, and relief filled him.

"It's a tree," he announced. "Dead fir, from the look of it."

The others approached, happy to see something that wasn't a threat.

Quonset held his lantern to the side. "There's another one, over there. . .and another. . . "

"It's a forest," Paradine realized, stepping a few paces forward. "They look to be pretty tightly packed."

"Forrester," Wills called. "How's the twine holding out?"

"About done, Captain."

"Got enough to tie it to this tree trunk?"

"Should be."

"Do it." He pulled a knife and carved a notch. "We'll mark the trees from this point in. Should be able to cover a good bit of ground that way. Jeb and Arty mighta found these woods and gone in. So, we'll give 'em the once over, then come back here and swing south, using the earlier plan."

"Fir forests can get pretty dense," Paradine said. "Could go for miles."

"I'm not looking to cover the whole thing," Wills replied. "Just enough to figure they're not in there."

With the line tied firmly to the tree, in they marched, their boots crunching against dead, dried, frozen needles. The light of their lamps faded as they moved deeper, vanishing into the eerie thicket.

Back at the edge of the clearing, darkness ruled once more.

"I think I like 'shadowy' better," said Michael.

"What, dear?"

" 'Shadowy.' I thought it said that, instead."

Lisabeth sat beside Michael, inside their wagon. "You thought *what* said that?"

"That part in the Bible you read the other day. " 'Though I walk through the valley of the shadow *of* death.' Only I thought it was 'shadowy death.' "

"Oh. . . " She put an arm around him. "Who told you it wasn't?"

"Daddy did. . .right before he went to find Mr. Lassiter and Mr. Sutton."

Lisabeth looked up and out into the surrounding void.

Lord, she prayed, *please bring him back to me, and open his heart so he can see You, there in the darkness that surrounds him. . .*

She glanced at the leather cover of the Bible, which was resting atop a storage chest.

. . .that has always *surrounded him.*

The men had put another hundred feet behind them. The woods were dense enough that it was relatively easy to see ahead and move from tree to tree, yet the trunks were spaced sufficiently that even their animals might have passed that way.

"How far we gonna go?" Garrett asked, waving his pistol. "I don't like being out here, not one bit. Something could be hiding behind every tree."

"Not much farther," Wills promised. "If these woods don't break soon, we'll turn back and search somewhere else."

"Arty?" Quonset called. "Jeb? You out here?"

Still no response.

"I say we turn back," Garrett said. "We already lost two; no sense in all of us dyin' for no good reason."

"That'll do, Asa," Wills said sharply.

"You saw what happened to Sam," he said. "What chance would *we* have if—"

"I said that's *enough!*" The captain elbowed the bearded pessimist, punctuating the command. "One more word outta you, and I'll send you back *alone*. You got that?"

Garrett grumbled what sounded like an obscenity, but Wills let it go.

"Captain," shouted Quonset, pointing ahead. "Looks like we're coming to a clearing. If so, how we gonna go any farther?"

"Let's see what we find," Wills said. "Then we'll figure it out."

"If anyone's interested," Paradine said, checking his watch by holding it near the glass of his lantern, "it's just past noon."

The forest ended, opening up as Quonset had presumed. Landmarks, however, would not be a problem for them here.

Tall pillars rose from the earth, separated by perhaps a dozen feet. There were many of them, straight and noble, their bright colors standing in stark contrast to the darkness beyond.

"Will you look at that," Paradine said, excitement in his voice.

"Totems." Wills smiled. "Northwest Indians. . .Nez Percé, maybe. At least we know someone's been here before us."

"No, I don't mean that," the teacher said, holding his light outward. "Look at the lanterns. . .how bright they are. . .how far the light carries! It's like *normal.*"

"He's right," Quonset chimed in. "A good twenty to thirty feet!"

It was true. The worst of the oppressive zone did not seem to exist on this side of the forest.

"Still freezing, though," Garrett said, hugging himself. "What I wouldn't give for a hot coffee right now."

"We must be onto something," Forrester said hopefully. "Could even be the way out. . .if the dark is letting up, there may be daylight just up ahead."

"Doesn't look like it," Wills noted. "Not from here, anyway."

The totem poles, they realized, faced away from them. Crossing to the other side of the sentry row, they came face to face with the images of Indian spirits, long forgotten.

"I've never seen these faces before," Paradine said, studying the carvings. "Don't look like they were carved by any of the tribes I'm familiar with."

"Does it matter?" Quonset asked.

"Just might have helped me figure out how long they'd been here, is all." He ran a hand along the eyelid of one of the carved and painted faces. "Chiseled from entire tree trunks. . .cedar, from the looks of them. Amazing craftsmanship."

Walking among the totems, Wills repeatedly called out the names of their missing friends and listened in the silence for an answer. None came.

"I don't think they came this way," he concluded. "We've seen no sign of 'em, and they could have headed in any direction once they left the camp."

"What about up ahead?" Forrester asked. "Do we keep going?"

"First priority is to find Arty and Jeb," the wagon master reminded him. "And we don't even know there *is* a way out ahead. Besides. . .we can't *walk* out of here, and there's no way the wagons are getting through those woods."

Quonset had taken several paces beyond the totems. "Captain, look at this."

Wills went to his side. Before them stretched a wide body of water, frozen solid and extending beyond their sight. Something caught the sentinel's eye—he knelt at the pebbled shore, holding his lamp near the surface. A trout was locked fast within the ice, its eyes glazed white, a wisp of blood trailing from its gills.

"Musta froze up quick to trap a fish right at the shoreline that way," he said. "How could it have happened so fast? This afternoon was a scorcher."

"Makes no sense," Wills scowled. "No sense at all."

"Lake, river, what?" wondered Quonset. "Whatever it is, I bet we could walk clear to the other side. I mean, look at it." He stepped out onto the ice, testing it with his full weight. "This is heavy midwinter ice. I'd be surprised if it wasn't several feet thick, all the way out."

"Could be," Wills nodded, rising to his feet, "but I sure don't know *how*. . . "

His words faded away as he noticed something far in the distance, out across the ice.

A light, small and steady. A lantern.

With a red lens.

"Well, I'll be a—"

Quonset saw it, too. "Wasn't there a minute ago. Didn't Jeb's boy say he was carrying a railroad lantern?"

"Sure enough."

Quonset stood up, swinging his lantern in an attempt to send a signal.

"Jeb!" he shouted. "Arty!"

No reply. The point of scarlet light remained motionless.

"Permission to take a party and check on it, sir?" the sentinel asked.

"I don't know," Wills said, reluctant to press that much farther onward. "Looks to be a good quarter-mile away."

"We can be there and back in no time."

The wagon master studied the distant light for a moment, then came to a reluctant decision. "We'll follow the shoreline, and—"

"If we do that, it could take *forever* to get there. We don't even know which direction the shore leads."

"All right," Wills agreed. "We'll go as the crow flies. But we spread out and take it slow, with the rope ready. . .just in case."

The others approached from behind, having heard Quonset's shouts. All eyes found the faraway light.

"S'pose that's really them, way out there?" Garrett smiled, rubbing his unkempt beard.

"Hope so," Quonset said. "We're gonna go find out."

"Across the ice?" Forrester asked.

"Yup. Besides, for all we know, the opposite bank may be only a hundred feet out, and they're camped beyond that, on solid ground."

Wills walked up to the schoolteacher. "Mr. Paradine, you and John wait right here. Keep your lamps bright so we can see 'em from out yonder. . .they'll have to guide us back."

"We'll be right here."

The two men watched as the others, separated by a safety cushion of a dozen feet, headed out across the ice. In moments, all that could be seen of them was their lanterns, swinging with each careful step.

"You wanted to go out there with them," Forrester said, lowering himself to the hard, cold soil. "Didn't you?"

"Thought maybe I could help."

The seated man shook his head and tossed a pebble out onto the ice. "Remember the Alamo."

Forward they marched, each step cautious, their eyes on the light ahead.

Wills was uneasy. Crossing ice was dangerous enough in broad daylight, let alone in the dead of night. Not that he had never done it before. One January night, years earlier, he and another soldier had saved one of their comrades who had fallen through a thin spot in a narrow Indiana river.

But this—?

"Watch each step," he warned. "Even if the ice holds, a fall can bang you up pretty good."

"We're on top of it, Captain," said Quonset, who had the lead a good fifteen feet ahead. Garrett, bringing up the rear, lagged an equal distance behind.

Wills turned to look over his shoulder. The shoreline behind them had receded from sight, but Paradine's and Forrester's lanterns still burned brightly there, shining like eyes, giving them an unmistakable twin homing marker.

So far, so good.

"We're about a hundred feet out," Quonset said. "Jeb's lamp doesn't seem any closer, though."

The wagon master's anxiety was growing. "Fellas, I *really* don't feel good about this."

"Opposite bank can't be *too* much farther," the sentinel said. "Let's give it about another fifty feet. See where we are then."

Garrett's eyes were trained downward, at the whiteness beneath him.

"Never seen ice like this," he said, "though I hear they get a lot of it up north. . .Lake Erie and such. Cousin of mine worked a barge there."

Another fifty feet passed. Then a hundred.

Still, the red light eluded them, seeming to draw no closer.

All around them, it became colder. Much colder.

"That's it," Wills called out, a deep anxiety shaking his voice. "We're turning back."

Quonset stopped and turned to face him. The uncharacteristic fear he saw in Wills' eyes shook him. "You all right, Jeremiah?"

"I just want off this ice is all," the captain said. "We go back and follow the shoreline around. Don't know why I let you talk me into this in the first place. I musta been crazy."

"Fine with me," Garrett said.

"Okay," Quonset nodded, yielding to his commander's wishes. "We'll head back."

They turned and focused on the two brilliant points now waiting for them, guiding them. One, two, three steps, Garrett now in the lead.

Something descended upon them.

Out of nowhere, a fierce polar blast roared downward, knocking all three men off their feet. Wills fell awkwardly, coming down on his elbow as his feet shot out from under him. He managed to cling to his lantern, but his rifle skittered away into the darkness. Intense pain wracked his body. He knew he had broken his arm, and badly. Struggling to his knees against the force of the wind, he saw the others also fighting to find their balance. He managed to raise his lamp.

Something malevolent moved within the dark wind.

"Crawl, if you have to!" he cried out, the words devoured by the gale. *"Keep moving!"*

As Wills watched, his eyes almost driven shut by the blasting wind, the ice under Garrett suddenly became fully liquid and the man plunged beneath the surface, vanishing from sight.

"Asa!" Wills screamed, moving forward, pulling the coil of rope from his belt. He spun toward Quonset. *"Asa's fallen through! We have to—"*

Quonset was not there. Water churned where he had once stood.

"Gordon!"

On his knees, Wills pushed against the wind, dragging his fractured arm, fighting to reach the sentinel.

He was mere feet away.

"I'm coming!"

With all his strength, he tossed the rope forward toward the water.

Too late. It fell upon solid ice.

What—?

He whirled. Where Garrett had been had also refrozen, instantly and impossibly, as thick and impervious as ever.

The winds ceased. As their roar subsided and faded away, Wills thought for an instant that he heard a deeper sound within them.

Laughter—?

On his knees where Quonset had been lost, Wills looked downward, his eyes wide. Crying out in fear and disbelief, he leaned over and slammed his good fist again and again into the unyielding surface, falling with the effort. Forcefully he wept, his face resting against the translucent, crystalline whiteness, the blows of his hand bloodying the frostbitten knuckles inside his leather glove.

Just beneath him, only inches away—yet beyond reach—Quonset stared sightlessly up at him, eyes wide in terror, mouth agape in a silent, eternal scream.

The two men had been entombed, locked into the ice.

◎ ◎ ◎

"I don't see their lights."

Paradine stood at the shore, watching for any sign of the men. Their lanterns had gone dark. Even the red light they had once seen had vanished.

"How long do we wait before we head back?" Forrester asked.

"I don't know. . .I hadn't considered it."

"Maybe they went around a bend, or over a hill. Who knows what the terrain is like out there."

"Maybe."

The schoolteacher returned to where Forrester sat leaning against one of the totem poles.

"I guess they'd still be able to see our lights," Paradine surmised, studying the brass lanterns resting at the shore. "They seem as bright as ever."

"I reckon so."

"We can't leave. What if we do, and they try to come back?

95

They'd have no way to find us."

Forrester nodded, doodling in the dirt with a small stick. "So. . .we wait."

Anxious minutes passed.

How long do *we wait?* Paradine wondered. *Hours? A day or more?*

"So, you're a schoolteacher?" Forrester asked. "I thought I heard Garrett call you that."

"Yeah." Paradine nodded. "A school back in Ohio. . .Bloom Township. Little one-room schoolhouse. . .it was my whole world. Seems a world away now. . . " He thought back, remembering the faces of the children, the joy of watching them learn.

"What about you?" he asked. "What'd you do, before all this?"

"I was a dentist. Lived in St. Louis." Forrester paused, and Paradine could see the memories flashing upon his face. "But then, my wife passed away. Her name was Emma. She meant everything to me. . . . "

"I'm sorry."

"It's okay. . .happened a few years ago now. Life goes on, isn't that what they say? Life goes on. Kept my practice for a while, but my heart wasn't really in it anymore."

"Understandable."

"Turned away from everything, after a while. . .even the church. They were kind enough and all, bringing food and saying how sorry they were about what happened, but I just. . ." He paused. The words were hard. "Haven't been much for church goin' since. Hurt to be there. . .she loved that place so much. Made me wonder what kind of God would take my Emma from me. Sort of had it out with Him one night. Haven't prayed since."

Paradine was uncomfortable with the subject. "So. . .why'd you join up with the wagon train?"

"With all the land being opened up out west, I thought maybe I'd make a fresh start. Maybe even find someone who'd have me, and raise a family. I'd really like to be a father. Always wanted a boy. Having a son means everything to a man. What I wouldn't give. . . " His voice trailed off.

"Well," Paradine gently said, "maybe one day you'll have one."

"You know," Forrester began, "I remember a time when—"

"Hold it," Paradine interrupted, his eyes trained ahead. "You see that?"

"What?"

Something was emerging from the darkness. It moved slowly, deliberately.

"It's the captain!" Paradine realized, leaping to his feet. Both men rushed onto the ice, meeting their leader a short distance out. The man had no lantern, no rope, no rifle. His gait was awkward. He cradled his arm. His face, devoid of expression, was somehow at the same time a mask of anguish.

"Captain?" he asked. "What happened? Where are the others?"

"Dead," Wills said flatly, his voice weak. "Both of 'em." He maintained his slow, forward stride, his eyes never leaving the twin lanterns.

"But. . .but what happened?" Forrester asked, meeting Paradine's eyes, sharing his alarm.

The wagon master kept plodding forward, without reply.

"Captain?"

"We better be gettin' back," he finally said.

When they reached the shore, Forrester went ahead and retrieved their lanterns, brushing the soil from their tarnished bases, and took a few steps toward the totems.

Wills, Paradine still at his side, paused at the edge of the ice.

He turned and looked into the teacher's eyes, as if to find answers there.

"Captain?" Paradine whispered. "What is it? What happened out there?"

Breaking eye contact, Wills slowly looked down at the ground between them. A puzzled Paradine followed his gaze.

There, within the ice, was the fish Quonset had discovered.

The two men's eyes met again. No further words were spoken. The captain stepped up onto the pebbled earth and headed for the tree line.

Chapter 6

The string is wiggling!

Billy Lassiter stood next to the wheel of his family's wagon, watching as the twine moved once more. He ran a finger gently along it, feeling the motion, knowing it might be his father's hand that, some distance away, was using the line to find his way home.

Billy's mother appeared at the rear of the wagon, her expression a mixture of fear and hope as she peered around the edge of her bonnet. Her red eyes betrayed the tears she had shed.

"Billy, you get back in this wagon this minute!"

"But, Mom—"

"Now!"

◎ ◎ ◎

Paradine, his hand riding the twine, took the lead, followed immediately by Wills and Forrester.

"Can't be too much farther," he said. "We passed the second knot a good distance back."

"I hope it's still tied where it's supposed to be," Wills said, obviously weary. Clutching his arm to his chest, with no spare hand with which to carry a lantern or follow the line, he shadowed Paradine, keeping only a step behind.

"Who would have moved it?" Forrester asked.

"Who would have killed our people?" he replied gravely. "Or tore up our wagons? Or taken our animals?"

"Point taken," Paradine said.

Suddenly, just at the edge of the throw of Paradine's lamp, Wills spotted something. He stopped abruptly, and Forrester walked into him.

"Ummph," the last man grunted. "Sorry, Captain. What is it?"

Paradine stopped, turned, and saw that the wagon master's attention had been drawn elsewhere. He held the lantern out in that direction, casting a little more light.

It was a fresh hole, unevenly dug as if by animals. Longer than it was wide, about the size of a man.

"A grave?" Paradine wondered.

"Last night," Wills confessed, "that's where we buried Johnny. Ground was frozen. . .went as deep as we could to keep the wolves from—"

"You sure this is the place?"

"I'm sure."

They stepped closer. Forrester and Paradine both held their lanterns out over the grave.

Empty.

Paradine looked at the strung line with new uncertainty.

"Let's go," he said, cocking his rifle.

◎ ◎ ◎

Lisabeth emerged from the wagon, her eyes frantically scanning the camp.

No, no. I told him not to—!

Voices rose only two wagons away. She heard a woman crying. She heard her husband.

Daniel!

She ran, homing in on the sound. Running around the rear of the schooner, she found in the lamplight the face she longed to see, one she had feared she never would behold again.

"Oh, Daniel!" she cried, falling into his arms, embracing him.

"I'm all right, Lis. . ."

The woman became aware of sobbing from her immediate left. Lassiter's wife, Judith, her face buried in a quilt, sat trembling in the back of her wagon. Just at that moment she had been told about Jeb.

"We didn't find Jeb," Paradine repeated to his wife, his tone grim. "Or Arty. And we lost Quonset and Garrett—"

"Daniel. . .it's *Michael*—"

"What? What about him?"

"He's disappeared. I haven't searched the whole camp yet, but I can't find him. I'm afraid he went ahead and—"

"And what?"

"He said he heard you calling to him from just beyond the wagons. . .said you wanted his help. I told him to stay put, but as soon as I turned around, he. . ."

Paradine closed his eyes. He was dead tired. His feet ached in his expensive boots. His stomach was growling audibly; his throat was parched for lack of water.

But his son was out there.

He spun to face Forrester, who was trying his best to console the grief-stricken Judith.

"He may just be lost," the dentist explained. "We weren't able to look everywhere. The way this dark knocks the light down, we—"

"In this place," the woman insisted, "lost is the same as dead."

"*Bunch* of folks have turned up missing," Lisabeth informed the two men. "Every time we turn around, someone else—"

"John," Paradine interrupted. "We have to go back out there."

"Ohhhhhh, no," the man said, shaking his head. "No, no, no. We barely got back. I'm not about to—"

"It's my son. . .he's wandered off. He's probably still close. . ."

Forrester winced. "You're *really* going back out there?"

Paradine's only answer was to grab a couple of pistols from atop a box in the wagon, check to make sure they were loaded, then hand one to him. Forrester drew a deep breath in frustration.

"I'm a *dentist,* for cryin' out loud."

"Having a son means everything to a man," Paradine said, using Forrester's own words.

Forrester swallowed hard.

Paradine checked his lantern's fuel, found it ample, then swung back toward his wife.

"Who's still here in the camp to protect you?"

"Eliza May's husband," she said, looking around. "And Mr. Langtree. . .oh, and Mr. Potter. A few others. . ."

"You stay in the wagon. I'll be back as soon as I can. Which direction did Michael go?"

"That way, I think," she pointed. "At least, he was looking over there."

Paradine checked his watch.

Three-seventeen in the afternoon.

He slipped into a belt and holster, and nestled the pistol there. Then, his rifle and lantern ready, Paradine leaned forward and kissed his wife.

"Don't you get yourself killed, Daniel Paradine," she said, trying to be brave.

"You can't get rid of me that easily." He smiled. " 'For better or for worse'. . .and this is the worse."

With a final, gentle nod, he broke into a run.

"Be careful!" Lisabeth called behind him. Then, more quietly, "Please, Daniel."

"Just call me blessed Davy Crockett," Forrester muttered, shoving the black powder revolver into his belt before once again taking up his rifle and his lantern. He headed off, close behind Paradine.

As her husband disappeared from sight, Lisabeth saw lanterns dancing not too far away. She just barely made out the forms of Wills being helped to his wagon by Billy Lassiter and Eliza May. The man seemed injured.

But he was alive, as was her husband.

Thank You for bringing Daniel back to me, she prayed silently. *Now, please—just once more—*

"He's gone," the new widow insisted. "Jeb's dead. . .just like them others. . . "

"We don't know that," Lisabeth said, reaching up to place a comforting hand on Judith's quilt-covered knee.

"Yes," Judith said. "I do."

◉ ◉ ◉

The man's gnarled old fingers trembled as they reached into the deerskin sack, seeking something they had not held for more than a year. He found the familiar wooden handle, smooth and worn, and a thousand memories rushed back, filling him at once with comfort, terror, and a deep sense of loss.

It had worked before. Now, he had heard the sounds again, the thunderous winds, the cries of pain.

The cruel laughter.

He looked at the long, deep scars running along the insides of his frail, mottled forearms.

Then, he had failed. The war had gone on.

But time had proven his defenses sure, his deeply held doctrine sound. He knew now what must be done.

◉ ◉ ◉

"We just went rushing back out here—"

"Michael!" Paradine called.

". . .no twine, no nothing. . ."

"Michael. . .answer me!"

". . .and now we'll never find our way back."

Resigned to the situation, Forrester held his lantern up, certain that each step forward was a step away from any possibility of survival. The frozen, brittle grass crunched beneath his boots.

"We'll get back," Paradine said, his tone determined. *"With* my son."

"I hope you're right, schoolteacher. . . . I'm not ready to be dinner for a pack of bears."

"Sleuth."

"What?"

"A *sleuth* of bears. . .not a pack. Unless they're polar bears."

"Really?"

"Yes. Why would I lie about that?"

"I guess you *are* a teacher," Forrester said, shaking his head, a slight smile crossing his lips despite his fear. "Who else would know such a thing?"

"People who read."

"*I* read. . ."

"I didn't say you didn't. You're a dentist—that must have taken a lot of study."

"You can say that again."

"Haven't been to one in years," Paradine confessed. "Just can't bring myself to sit in that chair. I wish there were a decent way to handle the pain. . . ."

"There is," Forrester said, allowing a measure of excitement to creep into his voice. "Fellow I met once in New York told me about a great anesthetic he's had a lot of success with. Something called nitrous oxide. . .works wonders, he said."

"Really?"

"Oh, yeah. Don't know why it works, but it sure does."

"I'll have to remember that next time I have a tooth pulled." He shouted again. *"Michael. . .it's Daddy. . . !"*

Forrester looked back over his shoulder. "I've lost the wagons, now. No sign at all. Sure hope you know what you're doing."

"I do, too."

"I didn't want to hear *that.*"

Their search continued, each minute seeming a much longer interval. Finally, something emerged from the darkness—a whitish form, low to the ground and almost skeletal.

"What. . .what is *that?*" Forrester stammered.

A few more steps and they had their answer.

A white, wooden cross. They had walked up on the back side of a grave.

Lanterns low, they moved around front. An epitaph became visible:

WILL MURPHY
FORGOTTEN BY GOD
1842

"'*42?*'" a stunned Forrester read. "That was fifteen years ago."

"Looks like this place has been drawing folks in for a long time," Paradine surmised. "Maybe even further back than that."

"What do you mean. . .'drawing them in'?"

"Nothing. . . . Just thinking out loud."

"Well, I'm staying with the sleuth theory."

"You know it isn't bears. Can't be."

"Yes, but I *want* it to be bears."

They thought to search for other graves. They did not have to go far.

The markers were everywhere, surrounding them, bearing silent witness that their deepest fears might not be unfounded.

"Look at that." Forrester pointed. "Bunch of 'em are dug up, just like Johnny's. *Most* of 'em, looks like. That one, and that one over there. . .and that one. . . "

"Could animals have dug so deep?"

"The bodies sure look to be missing. . . ."

"So why are these other graves still intact?" Paradine wondered. "Haven't been so much as touched. Markers aren't even knocked over."

Other names, other dates. Some of the hastily made markers were smashed and illegible, lying in splinters on the ground. The men examined them, one by one, calling them out.

"1841," Paradine read. "1854. . .1852. . . "

"1856," Forrester continued. "Another one, 1842. . ." He paused. "Dan. . .there's dozens of 'em. This is a graveyard."

"Look here," Paradine called, moving down the row. He held his light out, revealing an ornately carved marble headstone. A man's name was chiseled neatly into the veined surface, along with intricate roses and cherubs. The date of the man's death, however, written just beneath, had been scraped crudely into the stone as if with a simple, sharp implement.

"He must have been bringing it with him," Paradine realized. "Maybe in case he died on the trail. . .he didn't want to be forgotten because of a wooden marker that didn't last."

"That's pretty sobering."

"Horrible thing to be forgotten."

"Well, he wasn't," Forrester said, reading the pristine stone. "Carlton A. Brunell, 1847. Pleasure to meet you. We'll never know who you were, but at least we know your name, and where you wound up."

Paradine spun in a slow circle, walking along the row of graves and finding indications of others beyond. "Look at them all. . . must be dozens. . . "

As they moved on, Forrester spotted another form ahead. "Watch it," he warned, leveling his rifle as their lantern light reached out.

"Wagons." Paradine's eyes left the field of graves. "Bunch of them. But they're in bad shape. . .abandoned."

"They're not ours," the dentist said, "are they?"

"No. . . "

Paradine cocked his head and stood for a moment, listening intently.

"Michael!"

"Warn me before you do that!" snapped a startled Forrester. "It's *creepy* out here."

Paradine held his light inside the bed of one wagon. "Stripped clean. . . Everything a person might find useful is gone, and then some."

"So, where is everybody?"

"You have to ask that?"

"Yeah, right," Forrester groaned, with a shiver. "Never mind."

In the stillness, a sound caught Paradine's ear.

"John," he whispered. "Listen."

The two men froze, their attention focused through their ears. It was subtle, but it was there—slow, deep, even.

Something was *breathing*. Loud, wet, raspy.

Inhuman.

Neither moved. Neither dared to. As they stood, the air grew much colder around them. Painfully so. The scent of decay was faint on the edge of the breeze.

They remained motionless, each man straining to determine the direction from which the sound came, but they couldn't tell. Their cheeks went numb. Paradine's hand tensed on his rifle.

If I can just get a bearing—if I can figure out where it is—

Then, finally, mercifully, the sound ceased. The air warmed slightly. After several minutes of unbroken silence, Paradine spoke quietly.

"I think it went away. . . ."

"Why would it?" Forrester whispered. "Why would something just watch us for a while, then walk off?"

"Don't know. . ."

"Maybe it's full," Forrester suggested, regretting the words even as they left his lips. "Hey, I'm sorry. . . . I forgot—"

"It's okay."

Michael.

"Come on," he said. "Let's keep moving."

"But—"

"If it's going to kill us, it's going to kill us. Whether we're here, or back at the camp. . .nowhere's safe. Remember Sam Carter?"

"Yeah, okay."

They pressed on, walking amid the wagons. "There's no pattern to it at all," Paradine said, frustrated. "The way the damage falls. Some of these are fully intact, while others are a shambles, or smashed to pieces."

"Could be they fought against the things," Forrester offered. "Defended some wagons better than others."

"Maybe. . .but I don't get that impression."

As they turned a corner, Paradine a few steps ahead, Forrester tripped over a broken section of yoke tongue and fell hard onto the frozen ground. The glass of his lantern shattered, exposing his fingers to the flame as they accidentally slipped inside the lamp.

"John!" Paradine called, rushing back. "You all right?"

"Yeah," he replied, gently pulling his bloodied hand free as he sat up. Jagged chimney shards had scraped his fingers. "Got cut on the glass a bit. But I don't get it."

"What?" Paradine asked.

Forrester slowly slid his index finger back inside the lantern, placing it directly into the flame.

"What are you doing?" Paradine said with alarm, bending down to stop him.

"No, it's all right," the man insisted. "Look. . .it's not even warm." He pulled his finger clear, revealing no burn, no blister, no redness.

109

Paradine furrowed his brow. All reason had fled this place long, long before. Reaching out, he too stuck a finger into the flame. No heat.

"What in the world. . . ?"

Forrester, rubbing his unscathed digit, sat bewildered. "How can fire not burn? Even the *flames* are cold in this place."

"Well," Paradine said, standing erect once more, *"that's* good news, anyway."

"How is that good?"

"We know this isn't hell."

Chapter 7

. . .and deliver us from evil. for His name's sake."

Lisabeth Paradine, Eliza May Taylor, and Marjorie Carter huddled inside the Paradine wagon, terrified and cold, their lanterns barely restraining the darkness. The women sat with their legs tucked beneath them, their hands clasped in a circle of hope, their eyes closed. They spoke in turn, their voices trembling slightly, their prayers whispered.

". . .please, Father. . .see us through this time of trial. . ."

The others had all vanished into the night, unseen and unheard. There had been no screams, no sounds of attack. Wills, Billy Lassiter—men, women, children. What once had been fifty-three souls had dwindled to four.

"And protect us here in this valley of shadowy death," Lisabeth added, her son's face filling her mind's eye. "Bring our husbands, children, and friends safely back to us. . .be our shield and our armor. . .comfort us with Thy rod and Thy staff. . ."

Judith Lassiter sat at the rear of the wagon, her arms crossed, her face fixed in a scowl.

"Don't bother," she said. The other women opened their eyes and looked at her.

"Even if there *is* a God," Judith went on, "He sure isn't in *this* godforsaken place. We're on our own, and we're never going to make it out alive."

"You don't know that," Eliza May said, nervously kneading the skirt of her dress.

"What makes *us* so special?" snapped the bitter, frightened woman. "Did my husband deserve to die? Or all of yours? Or our babies. . . ?"

"My husband isn't dead," Lisabeth held firm. "He'll be back."

"Of course he will," Judith mocked. "He's too *smart* to die."

"That's enough," Marjorie said. "Nothing makes us special. . . nothing ever has. But Christ *is* special, and we're His. And whatever happens, we trust Him."

Judith laughed.

"What about you?" she asked Eliza May. "Just a little while ago, you were spouting off about the end of the world!"

"I was scared," she replied. "I still am. . . . But like she said, we trust God."

"If it isn't our time," added Lisabeth, "we *will* live through this."

"Without Jeb and my son," Judith said, angry tears overflowing, "I don't *want* to."

● ● ●

Rounding one of the wrecked wagons, Paradine kicked aside a small, open wooden chest, breaking loose the lone hinge that held its lid. As it tumbled, the contents spilled—a rusted knife, a bullet mold, a pair of glasses with one lens missing, and a little hardbound book. The red leather binding caught his eye—he hung his lantern on the broken spoke of a wagon wheel, stooped down, and picked it up.

"What is it?" Forrester asked, walking up from behind.

Paradine flipped a few pages. "It's a journal. Someone was keeping a diary of their trip."

"What's it say?"

"Starts in Missouri," he replied after a moment, scanning the first page. "May 4, 1854. He complains about how much he had to spend on gunpowder. His spelling's atrocious."

"Toward the end, I mean. About *this* place."

Paradine skipped to the back, studied a few of the hand-written leaves, and selected a place to begin.

"Don't know what day it is," he read, having to guess at some of the words. *"Several died the first night. . .looked like animals had set upon us, but now we know better. Frank lost his boy. . .he's taking it hard and stays off to hisself. Circling the wagons didn't make no difference. . .whatever is attacking us has no fear and comes right into the camp. But we never see a thing. It never shows itself. It hides in the dark. Katrina says it's the devil hisself, and I'm not sure she's far wrong."*

He jumped ahead a few pages.

"Not many left now. Don't know why it doesn't just finish us off. No animals left. Found some of our oxen a few hours ago. . .just like before, their insides were et out. Bones scattered everywhere. . .like

113

what's left of a chicken after Sunday dinner."

Forrester cringed.

"Just us two left, now. We buried my precious Annabelle yesterday. The cholera finally took her. . .at least she's free of this terrible place. She looked so much like her mother. . .so beautiful. . ."

The words were not easy to read. Paradine paused, gathering himself.

"The water barrels are all froze up now. Didn't happen for days, so why all of a sudden? Tried to thaw the ice a bit, but even the campfire flames are cold. . ."

"No water," Forrester groaned. "I didn't think of that. A man can't last long without it. We could be in trouble."

"Doesn't have to be liquid. Ice works fine. . .you can chip it up and eat it. Worse problem is freezing to death."

"Yeah, I guess so."

He flipped a few more pages.

"The handwriting changes, right at the end," Paradine noted. *"Vince got killed today. Same as the others. . .all tore up. Buried him next to his daughter. Ground's too hard to go deep. Don't guess it matters. Just me now."*

"Then what?"

"That's where it stops."

Both men whirled as a new sound began to rise—distant and faint, but steady and rhythmic.

"You hear drumbeats?" Forrester asked. "Or am I going crazy?"

"Yes," Paradine said, peering into the dark, homing in. "I hear them. Coming from that way. . .I'd bet my life on it."

"You may well be."

"Come on," he said, retrieving his lantern. "We're going to find it."

"I don't think that's a good idea," Forrester said, standing his ground. "Drums usually mean Indians. What if somehow they're behind all this?"

"What if they're not?"

"We could be walking into a trap."

"We're in a trap *now,* John," Paradine said. "Listen. . .those drums are the closest thing to a guidepost we've had since we got here, and Michael's bound to hear them, too. He's got to be as lost as we are—"

"You said we weren't lost."

"—and he's bound to go in search of them, so that's what *I* intend to do. You coming with me, or not?"

"Well, we've come *this* far," Forrester sighed. "Might as well see the *entire* nightmare."

The pounding of the drums continued. The two men found themselves marching to its beat as more and more distance fell behind them.

"Getting louder," Paradine noted. "We're moving in the right direction."

"Terrific."

"I just hope it doesn't stop. . . . That could be trouble. If we should lose our bearings *now*. . ."

A familiar sight emerged before them.

"The trees again," Forrester realized. "We're headed back toward that lake where Garrett and—"

"Stands to reason," Paradine said, cutting him off. "*If* it's the same woods as before. For all we know, we could be moving in the opposite direction. But if you're right, and considering the totem poles we saw earlier—"

"Then it *is* Indians."

"Probably."

"And that doesn't worry you?"

"No," the teacher said. "Not if they're the ones that carved those totems."

"Why not?"

"Those were made by a Northwest tribe. Don't know which one. . .could have been any number of them. But they're not like the Snake Indians, or the Apaches, or the Cheyenne. . .they have no real beef with us. Not yet, anyway, as far as I know."

"You aren't sure."

"I'm just saying it isn't likely. But there's a bigger issue at stake here."

"Such as?"

"If someone still lives here, they must have something keeping them alive. . .some protection from that thing we don't know about. And that protection may be the only chance we have. . . all of us."

"Assuming the *thing* isn't what's beating that drum right now," Forrester winced. "Could be a dinner bell—and we're the dinner."

"Well, then," Paradine smiled, "I say we keep a good thought and find out."

"Lead on," Forrester conceded, pulling his knife. He cut a slash into the first tree he passed, then another, alternating with Paradine. The woods seemed a bit thicker than those they had seen before. The undergrowth was more dense, though dead and brittle. Forward they drove, stepping high, their boots making more noise than they would have liked.

"We're sure not sneaking up on anybody," Paradine said.

"Works both ways," Forrester noted. "We'd hear *them*, too."

"Hope so."

The drum grew steadily louder. Finally, the forest ended and, as before, they stepped out into a clearing.

"We in the same place?" Forrester asked.

"Could be," Paradine guessed, looking at the ground. "Looks similar. We might just be farther along in one direction or the other." He paused to listen. "That way," he pointed, departing the tree line at an angle. "We're really close now."

Step after cautious step, beat after beat, they moved forward. Phantoms seemed to flutter at the limits of their peripheral vision, drawing their attention time and again, yet nothing was ever there.

"Our lanterns seem brighter," Forrester said, fighting to remain hopeful. "Like before. Good sign. . ."

A hundred feet later, familiar forms appeared.

"The totems," Paradine said. "We're back where we were."

It was true. Before them stretched the frozen lake. At a point along the tree line almost a hundred feet to their right was the path they had forged earlier.

The drum, however, sounded to their left, from an area they had neither seen nor explored on their first visit. With some reluctance, they turned from the familiar scene, pressing deeper into the unknown.

They did not have to go far.

"It's a house," Paradine said as a long wooden structure became visible. "And another beyond that. . ."

"So, it isn't Indians, then," the dentist said with renewed hope.

"No, no. . .it *is*," he whispered. "Northwest tribes don't make teepees. They build wooden houses." The scholar in him was amazed as he held his lantern near the support post of an outer wall. "Never thought I'd see one up close. . .what craftsmanship! This carved detail is—"

"Can we stay focused here, please?"

They passed a second house, then a third. All were dark, with no sign of life within. The lake lay only twenty feet away—on its shore rested a pair of dugout canoes, twenty feet in length and covered in artistic carvings. At their bows rose large, stylized representations of the heads of birds, brightly colored and polished smooth.

The drum grew still louder. Paradine and Forrester turned a corner—and stopped dead in their tracks.

From the next house, warm, dancing light spilled from an open doorway, carrying upon its shoulders the percussion, as well.

They set their lanterns on the ground, then brought their rifles up and cocked them. Quietly approaching, they pressed themselves close to the front of the house, slid along the façade, and edged up to the doorway.

They listened.

A voice. Rhythmic and repetitive, weak but steady.

Taking a deep breath, his heart pounding in his chest as the drum pounded in his ears, Paradine leaned just enough to get a glimpse inside.

His eyes fell upon the figure of a man—a very *old* man, sitting cross-legged on the floor, bathed in firelight. His face was hidden by a grotesque, wooden mask with painted eyes and a threatening expression. His hair was pure white and hung beyond his shoulders. His frail form was draped in leather, his chest covered by an ornate breastplate crafted of wood and bone. His mask muffled the phrase he continually uttered as the leather-headed tom mallet in his right hand struck the drum in his lap again and again.

Paradine pulled back.

"What is it?" Forrester whispered.

"A medicine man, I think. Seems to be alone. I don't think he can see. . .he's wearing a ceremonial mask."

"What do we do?"

"We go in."

Drawing courage from a breath, Paradine stepped fully into the doorway, rifle drawn, with Forrester immediately behind him. Slowly, they crossed the threshold.

The tread of Paradine's boot on the plank flooring was met with a squeak of straining wood.

The drumming stopped. The old man went still.

Paradine and Forrester froze, their eyes on the seated figure.

He reached up and pulled his mask away, revealing a lined face with angular features. Though reflecting the features of an Indian of the Pacific Northwest, he was more pale than Paradine had expected. He wore a white beard and mustache, untrimmed and untamed. His eyes, gray and weary, looked at the strangers without fear.

He said nothing.

Paradine stepped deeper into the room. Forrester, more cautious, maintained more distance.

"Indians don't have beards," he muttered under his breath.

"They do up here," Paradine corrected him.

The two men scanned the room. Elaborate woven hangings surrounded them, separated by expanses of reddish, polished wood. Pieces of pottery, both functional and decorative, lined a series of shelves, along with small wooden statues of people, birds, and beasts. Animal skins, losing their fur in mottled patches, covered the floor almost from wall to wall. Carved ornaments hung from the overhead beams, catching the light of the fire, which burned brightly beneath an iron cauldron. The smell of cooking meat filled the air, and two neglected stomachs growled in response.

The men realized the room was *warm*.

The aged man made no threatening move. He watched the

two strangers as if waiting for something. Paradine and Forrester looked at each other—the latter nodded in the Indian's direction and shrugged.

Paradine crouched low, hoping to appear less imposing.

"My name is Daniel Paradine," he said, his eyes locked on those of the old man. "This is John Forrester. We're trapped here. . .I'm looking for my son."

Nothing.

"I don't think he speaks English," Forrester surmised.

"I didn't think he would," Paradine said, cleaning his glasses on the sleeve of his shirt. "But now that that's out of the way. . ."

He repeated the words in an Indian language, hoping the words would be generic enough to prompt a response.

Again nothing.

"If we can't talk with him, he's not going to be much help," said the dentist.

All right, Paradine decided, *we'll start with the basics—*

He gestured with one hand as if eating, and rubbed his stomach.

The Indian watched Paradine, then glanced at Forrester, who mimicked the first man's motions. After a moment, he set his drum aside and tried to stand. The teacher moved forward, helped him to his feet, and watched as the ancient man walked with some difficulty toward the fire.

The awkward gait drew the men's attention downward. Barely visible below the hem of the man's leather robes was the club foot that had hobbled him for almost seven decades.

He filled two pottery bowls with the soup simmering in the pot and handed them to the visitors. The pair sat on the floor and began to sip from them.

"Rabbit, I think," Paradine said, pulling chunks of meat from the bowl with his fingers.

"Where'd he get a rabbit? Nothing's alive out there."

"Beats me. . .but it's a great question."

The old man offered bowls filled with water.

"Sweet," Forrester added, gulping it down. "Best I ever tasted."

Their host returned to his place on the floor. After a moment, staring forward, he spoke once more but nothing in his words or gestures yielded a clue as to his meaning. Paradine listened, hoping to catch something—anything—that might allow him to open an avenue of communication.

"He talking to us?" Forrester asked, sipping from his bowl.

"I don't think so," Paradine guessed, watching the Indian closely. "Seems more like a chant of some kind."

"Any ideas?"

"Nothing," the scholar said in frustration. "Must be some sort of dialect. Doesn't sound like anything I've ever heard. Not even close. I thought maybe—"

A few syllables struck Paradine's ear as familiar.

"Can't be. . . ," he whispered.

"What?" Forrester asked. "What is it?"

"That one word sounded. . .*French.*"

"Is that possible?"

"Maybe. . ." Paradine set his soup bowl on the floor and moved closer to the old man. He held his breath, then tried a long shot. *"Parlez vous Francais?"*

The Indian halted his chant, turned, and looked into Paradine's eyes. For a few moments, he said nothing. Then, he looked away, his eyes darting as if long-buried memories were being mined.

Come on, Paradine urged silently.

The old man's gaze met the teacher's once more.

"*Oui,*" he said.

"Yes!" Forrester cheered.

Paradine smiled widely and began anew, speaking in French.

"I am Daniel Paradine," he began. "This is John Forrester. We are searching for my son. . .he is lost in this place."

"If he is lost here," the old man said, "he is truly lost."

"Ask him how we get out of here," Forrester urged.

"I'll get to that. . .first things first."

"Gettin' out of here seems pretty *first* to me."

Paradine continued, speaking slowly. His own French was a little rusty—it had been years since he had practiced it, and then only sparingly.

"Do you have a name?"

"Seukani," he replied.

"Tell me, Seukani. . .what is happening in this valley? Why is it so dark and so cold? What is killing our families and our livestock?"

The Indian at first seemed reluctant to answer.

"Chayatocha," he whispered, averting his eyes. "It is Chayatocha."

"Is that the *name* of something?" Paradine asked, unsure. "What is this *Chayatocha?* What does it want?"

"It is the great, devouring spirit, most wicked and very powerful. It has walked from the birth of the world. It is forever hungry, and feeds on all things. . .the fire, the sky, the beasts, the lands, and we who live upon them."

That's a little more than I was expecting—

Paradine looked to Forrester, his expression grim.

"I don't know French," the dentist said. "What did I miss?"

"He says that it's an evil spirit. . .something that devours everything."

"Terrific." He leaned back against the wall. "Go on. . .just fill me in when you're finished."

The teacher turned back to the old man. "How do you know this?"

"It was told to me when Chayatocha first fell from the skies, and the eternal night descended. The legends had been handed down. . .and they were true."

"When did this happen?"

"I was a boy then. It was. . .long ago."

"In all these years, why hasn't this Chayatocha hurt you?"

"Because I use the ancient magic, taught to me by our medicine chief before he disappeared. . . ." He indicated the drum. "Through it, the life spirits protect me, and feed me, and bring me water."

"How?" Paradine asked.

"Food is left at my door each day, and has been since the animals and fruit trees all perished. Chayatocha killed them all, as well as my tribe, including my beloved mother. But never has it touched *me*—it roars and continually threatens to attack, but it is held at bay."

Paradine looked at the scars cut deeply into the man's forearms. "Then how did you get those wounds?"

"There was a time," Seukani recalled, his voice low, "when I no longer wanted to live. I could not bear the loneliness, nor the constant torments of Chayatocha. I tried to end my own life, using a knife, and fell into the final sleep. But then I awoke, and found I had been healed. . .and I knew the life spirits wished me to remain."

The teacher paused for a few moments, considering all he had heard.

"There have been others, like us," he said at last. "We are in search of a land west of here. A great many have passed this way."

"I know of this," the old man said. "And I have fed them, and have given them a place to sleep. At first, when they began to come, I was joyful to see them. . .to have my solitude put aside. But Chayatocha always finds them here, and takes them for itself, and devours them."

"Always?"

"All who have come here have not lived long." He paused, as if reluctant to go on. "It will find you, too. . .and I will be alone again. I am sorry."

There was a harsh silence.

"Why do the spirits protect only you?"

"I do not know."

Figures—

"That thing out there. . .is there a way to destroy it? Does your magic speak of *anything?*"

"No, nothing of which I am aware, but there is much I do not know. If I *had* known of such a thing, I would have tried it long ago. All I can do is please the life spirits, and they protect this house."

So much for that—

"Listen," Paradine said, "I am looking for my son. His name is Michael. He is young—eight years old. Dark hair, brown eyes. Has he been here?"

"No. But I know where he may be."

Paradine's eyes widened. "Where?"

"Where all of our children were taken, except for me." With Paradine's help, Seukani struggled to his feet and led the men toward the door.

"Where are we going?" Forrester asked, rising.

"He says he knows where Michael might be."

They followed the elderly man outside. After a moment, he stopped and pointed up and into the distance.

"There," he said, his breath fogging. "On the mountain. . .the place of Chayatocha."

As they watched, a light appeared—dull orange and flickering slightly, as if a fire burned.

"The light returns," Seukani said, with some surprise. He looked at Paradine with sadness in his eyes. "I have not seen it in a long time."

"What does it mean?" Paradine asked fearfully.

"Chayatocha is expecting you."

Michael—are you up there?

"What is that, a cave?" Forrester asked, deaf to the old man's words. "Looks like it's up in the sky."

"Have you been up there before?" Paradine asked the Indian.

"Never. When I was younger, I was afraid. Now, I am too old and too weak."

"How do you know that's where the children were taken?"

"Long ago, when a few of us remained, we saw the light as you do now. Some of our people went there in search of our missing. Only one brave returned, wounded and dying, and he told us what he had seen."

Paradine briefly told Forrester all he had learned. The dentist turned again and watched the glow on the mountain.

"I'm sorry, Dan," he said, "but if you're going up there, I just can't go with you. It'd be like walking into the jaws of the *thing*, and. . .I'm just not up to it."

"It can find you no matter where you are, if what the old man says is true."

"I know, but. . ." He hung his head. "I can't go any farther. I just can't. Maybe at one time, but. . .when I lost Emma, I lost a lot of myself. I just. . .I'm sorry."

Paradine nodded, realizing he was on his own, knowing he had no right to ask a man to risk his life for another man's son.

"It's all right, John."

As Paradine walked back into the house to retrieve his weapons, Forrester brought the lanterns from where they had left them.

"You stay here," Paradine said, taking his lamp. "Stay inside. I'll be back. . .with Michael."

"I know you will," Forrester said. Ashamed, relieved, and worried, he reached out and hugged the teacher. "You get yourself back here as soon as you can."

"Count on it."

A final pat on the back, and Paradine turned toward the light.

Forrester watched him vanish into the night, knowing he would never see him again.

Chapter 8

The way was hard, the path rocky. Paradine pressed onward and upward, burdened by the awkwardness of the rifle in his hand. Managing both it and the lantern was difficult, for the climb demanded at least one free hand for balance as he leaned on boulder after boulder along the way.

Always, the light of the lair shone down, mocking his feeble attempt at rescue.

He found petroglyphs on some of the large stones, images of men and animals engaged in the hunt. Clearly, they predated the coming of whatever awaited him above.

Hours passed. The going became more difficult. The air grew thinner, colder. More than once, he paused to catch his breath, knowing he was likely seeing his last moments of life.

Finally, he crested a ledge and found the entrance to a cavern only a few dozen feet away. As he drew near, he began to realize the horror that awaited him.

The desiccated bodies of two of Seukani's tribal brothers, presumably two who had once dared confrontation, stood sentry at the mouth, one to either side. Pointed beams of wood, thrust into their rib cages, propped up their now-meager corpses. Eyeless sockets stared outward, mouths gaping open in silenced screams. In their gnarled hands they held the weapons they had carried in life, stone-tipped spears once used for the hunting of game.

A sulfurous scent poured from the cave, repulsing Paradine. Fighting to keep his focus and not flee in fear, he held his lantern high and entered, following the amber glow.

◎ ◎ ◎

Forrester watched as the tiny point of white light disappeared into the mountainside.

He made it.

The dentist from St. Louis hated himself for his cowardice. Once, there had been an inner strength he had drawn upon, long before. But now, by choice, he walked alone.

"I'm so sorry, Dan," he said, looking away, looking inward. "You deserved better. No man should have to die alone."

"Venir a l'interieur, ou c'est chaud," called the old man from inside the house.

Forrester turned and walked out of the darkness into the warm light.

◉ ◉ ◉

The cavern floor was slippery. A damp, heavy cold encompassed him, numbing his face and his hands, despite the gloves. The dull, ominous light seemed to come from everywhere, as if the walls themselves bore an unearthly radiance. Some areas seemed more ice than stone, as if deep, glowing cavities or side passages had been sealed over. He brought his rifle up, cocked it, and tensed for battle.

Deeper he moved, his swinging lantern throwing moving shadows that seemed like crawling, living things. It felt as if the cave were closing in around him.

The entrance tunnel soon widened, opening into a literal chamber of horrors.

The cavity was more than fifty feet wide, with a ceiling that arched some thirty feet above. It was rough, as if excavated by hand. Icicles hung like crystalline stalactites.

Lowering his gaze, Paradine froze.

Massive piles of bones lined the walls, the remains both human and animal. Ten feet high the piles soared, representing the deaths of hundreds, if not thousands, of individuals. There was a sheen on the bones that caused them to catch the light in dramatic and sickening fashion.

More ice.

Paradine approached one of the piles, examining a few of the bones more closely.

It can't be—

Strange cuts and scrapes covered them from end to end, but Paradine could see they had not been made with a blade. After a moment, he realized what they were.

Tooth marks—!

He backed away slightly, struggling against the rising bile in his throat as he turned, swinging his light in a different direction. It caught a glimmer in the distance, across the way—a treasure trove of objects of antiquity, a king's ransom. From his biblical studies and his history texts, he knew what they were and their places of origin—and he was astounded.

This can't be—it just can't—!

Piled high before him were the riches of the ages.

Wooden chests, covered in gold.

Egyptian?

Tablets of clay and stone, inscribed with writings.

Babylonian?

Carved figurines of people and animals, inlaid with silver, gold, and jade.

Greek? Roman? Chinese?

Most he recognized as having come from the Middle East and Asia. Others, he did not know at all. Every single piece, however large, however small, would have been prized by every museum in the world.

Another pile held more recent items of American origin— clocks, weapons, pocket watches, china, silverware, musical instruments, and jewelry.

No doubt where those *came from,* Paradine mused.

Astonished, he turned, casting his lamplight across the cavern toward a third area behind him.

There waited the object of his quest.

Startled, he jumped, almost dropping his lantern. For an instant, his mind boggled, threatening to shut down altogether. His heart leapt against his rib cage.

Before him, face-to-face, was Death—it had to be! More frightening than any scythe-carrying, robe-wearing, skeletal

130

invention of man, it sat nestled on a pile of bones like an emperor on a throne—a shape of unimagined darkness, its yellow eyes glowing. The aura of night that surrounded it flowed around its form like a garment, rippling like fabric in a breeze, concealing it, hiding it from human eyes. The very air froze upon contact, sending a continual rain of ice dust onto the pile of bones and the floor. Its arms spread wide as it lounged, its shoulders spanning more than six feet. Patiently, it watched Paradine with seeming amusement.

It had been behind him the entire time.

Trembling, the schoolteacher stepped back, his rifle aimed squarely.

Watery, jaundiced eyes blinked a few times as they examined the intruder. A voice boomed forth, echoing from the glistening, blood-marred walls, deep and guttural, its quality not that of a single voice but seemingly that of a thousand, all speaking in unison. A voice of intellect, power—eternity.

"What do you want here?"

Paradine, his heart racing, stood his ground—yet words would not come.

"Cat got your tongue?"

"I think you know why I'm here," he finally said defiantly.

"Do we?"

He could not look away.

"A visitor. . .we receive so few," the being continued, its voice heavy with sarcasm. *"Welcome to the valley of the shadowy death."*

It had heard. *Michael!*

"Where's my son?" Paradine demanded.

With a crunching of bones, the being shifted its weight.

"Please," it mocked, eyeing the rifle, *"do not harm us."*

Paradine moved to the side, closer to the cavern entrance.

His weapon remained leveled. "What have you done with him?"

"How far your kind has fallen," the voice boomed. *"You once were a fairly respectable race. . .now you are but a shadow. We will never understand what he sees in you."*

"He. . .who?"

"Do you not know?"

"You speak English," Paradine realized.

"We command every language of man," it said with pride. *"Lei ci dubita? Hemos visto las cosas que usted no ha soñado de. . .wir sind zu jeder Ecke der Welt gereist. . ."*

"Have you now?" Paradine asked, understanding the common European languages. "Unimpressive, I must say."

It smiled at his insolence, then uttered what seemed to be a soliloquy, in a tongue of amazing beauty and tonal complexity, one the scholar never had heard. Paradine stared silently, lacking for a response.

"Your ears have borne witness to words not spoken in millennia," it gloated. *"A tongue now known only to us, and otherwise remembered only by great, forgotten temples and monuments of limestone. . . the language of ancient Egypt."*

"That's impossible. . ."

"No living man has heard it. . .save you, of course."

Paradine stood amazed, fighting the urge to beg for more.

It reached over and picked up the remains of an arm, with the wrist and hand still attached by dried, frozen ligaments.

"Normally, we would have destroyed you by now, as we did the others."

"Why haven't you then?" He shook the rifle slightly. "Because of this?"

It shook its head, and the walls rattled with thunderous laughter. *"A toy."*

With the crack of crushed bone, it *rose*. Pulling itself to its full stature, it towered above Paradine, a living wall more than ten feet high.

Paradine took an involuntary step backward, gathering his courage.

"My son," he demanded. "Where is he?"

"Patience." It moved toward the pile of antiquities. Paradine felt the impact of each step in the stone floor beneath him. *"Do you admire our trinkets? Call it a weakness of ours. They are reminders of past. . .relationships."*

Suddenly, the thing whirled and with incredible speed ripped the rifle from Paradine's grip. From the momentary contact, his right hand was almost frostbitten. He slipped it under his coat, trying to warm it.

"Unimpressive," the thing commented, examining the rifle. It looked along the sight, peered into the barrel, and ran a finger along the stock before tossing it casually onto the pile of more recent acquisitions. *"But we will keep it as a remembrance of your visit."*

The being moved to where Paradine was standing and bent down to face him, eye to eye. The man fell back onto the bones behind him and tried hard not to scream. As the thing pressed close, its rasping breath splashed him, cold and smelling of a slaughterhouse. At such proximity, Paradine could see that it did indeed have a face—not quite human, but a seeming corruption of humanity. Pinned there, he turned his face aside, his eyes closed as if to shut out the terror that swept him.

"Pray that you die quickly," it said. *"Drop to your knees. . .let us hear you pray."*

"I don't pray," Paradine said, quivering. "I can take care of myself."

"Can you now. . . ?"

The man trembled, struggling not to show his fear.

"We have only to touch you," it said, *"and your life ends."*

"Then do it," Paradine said defiantly, finding a courage that surprised him, "or get away from me."

It smirked, pulling back slightly, and again broke into a bellowing laugh. *"We like you. You intrigue us. . .as you have from the beginning. Few have done so. . .and they were long ago and far away."*

"Lucky me."

The thing's hand shot forward, ripping the spectacles from Paradine's face in a lightning movement. He felt the searing cold against his forehead. By the time his reflexes could react, it was over. He watched as his eyeglasses were tossed onto the pile, their lenses and frames covered in frost.

In amazement, he realized he had *seen* his glasses being tossed.

"No longer will you need those crude implements," the being said. *"You will behold our magnificence with your own eyes."*

It was true. Paradine looked around the room—everything was in perfect focus.

"I've worn glasses since before I can remember," he said, unable to believe his eyes.

I can see—I can really see—!

"Why?" Paradine challenged.

"A token of our power."

The creature returned to its seat on the bone pile. *"We can read you. . .we know your thoughts. You are not like the others who have come into this valley, all weak of mind and ignorant of the past. You are one who knows and appreciates the history of this world, and you are worthy of the honor we will do you. You will witness firsthand glories seen by no living man."*

Paradine backed away, his eyes locked upon the thing.

"What are you?" he asked. "Where did you come from?"

"You shall have your answer."

"How did you bring us here? What did you do to our scout?"

"He was an empty house."

"What about the others?" he dared to ask. "Why did they deserve to die? You killed my friends. . . ."

"My apologies," it said with mock regret. *"What must we have been thinking? Would you like to take them with you?"*

It reached into the pile upon which it rested and pulled something free, something momentarily concealed in the palm of its immense, taloned hand.

"This one amused us," it said, tossing the object to Paradine. The man made no attempt at a catch, but instead let it land dully at his feet, where it bounced slightly and came to rest.

He looked down at the gnawed skull and in horror recognized the distinctive dental work, the glint of gold.

Jeb Lassiter.

Paradine fell back in revulsion.

"Oh, forgive us," the beast said. *"Are you two not getting along?"*

Derisive laughter echoed from the walls of the chamber.

Angrily, Paradine pulled a pistol from his belt—*Lassiter's* revolver—and fired it at the creature, emptying the six-shooter with no noticeable effect. As the echo of the gunshots died away, the thing waggled a finger at him.

"Come now. . .did you really think to kill *us?"*

Defeated, Paradine threw the spent gun aside. It clattered loudly against the floor.

"On the pile, please," the thing said, sarcastically scolding him. *"This is our home, after all."*

"Where is my son?" Paradine demanded yet again.

"If you want to see him again, you will return to us tomorrow night when we summon you, and we will show you things no living man has seen."

"Why should I trust you? What if I *don't* come back?"

"Then we will kill you. We will visit your camp and. . .amuse ourselves."

"That won't be necessary," Paradine said, hoping to protect his family and the others.

"See that it is not."

"If I come back, will you leave everyone else alone?"

"You would bargain with us?" it suddenly roared, smashing its fists into the throne and splintering bone, startling the man anew. *"We take what we will and do what we will!"*

"All right!" Paradine conceded. "All right. Just tell me. . .how am I supposed to return to my camp? Will you lift the darkness that covers the area beyond the forest?"

"That I will not do. But I have imparted to you a certain knowledge of the lay of the land, enough to get you there and back." It looked away. *"Now, go. . .you are becoming tiresome. Leave here before I change my mind."*

As angry as he was frightened, Paradine backed away and headed toward the entrance of the cave.

Seukani looked up as the door opened.

"You are back," he said with a measure of surprise. "Never before has any man walked into the lair of Chayatocha and returned unharmed. Perhaps the life spirits are keeping you safe as well."

"Sure wasn't on account of anything *I* did, believe me. I was lucky to get out of there."

"Did you find your son?"

"No," Paradine said, grim-faced, setting his lantern on the floor, "but he was promised to me."

"A promise from such as Chayatocha carries no weight," the old man said quietly.

"I'm well aware of that."

The old man brought water and watched as the teacher drank.

"You may stay here with me, if you wish," Seukani offered. "I would welcome the company."

"I can't. I'm sorry. I have to get back to my family and the others."

The Indian nodded.

"Where's John?" Paradine asked, looking around the room. "The man who was with me?"

"He is not here."

"Where did he go?"

"I do not know. I slept, and when I awoke, he and his things were gone."

"It wasn't. . .I mean, Chayatocha didn't. . .did it?"

"I do not know."

Paradine scowled. "If he should return, tell him I was here. Tell him I went back to the camp."

"I will do so."

They embraced. The elderly Indian handed his visitor a small pouch of dried rabbit meat.

"For the journey." He smiled.

"Thank you."

"Please," Seukani said, his eyes wet, "visit me again."

Paradine nodded, picked up his lantern, and departed into the night.

Chapter 9

Paradine crossed through the forest and onto open ground. He was amazed—suddenly, almost instinctively, he knew where he was and where he was headed. Every tree trunk, every blade of dried grass seemed familiar to him. The outbound journey, stumbling in the dark, had taken hour upon hour. Now, heading straight back, he covered the distance in one-tenth the time.

He bypassed the cluster of broken wagons and the graveyard, for they lay out of the way, he now knew. He hurried on, following a direct path.

The camp appeared ahead. "Lisabeth!" he called, moving forward at a dead run.

He slowed his pace as what he was seeing began to sink in.

Most of the wagons had been destroyed, reduced to heaps of wood, metal, and shredded fabric. There was no sign of anyone. All of the livestock was gone. Blood was splattered on a few of the wagons and the ground around them, yet there were no bodies.

"Lisabeth!" he cried, more frantically now. He ran the circumference of the camp, passing one shipwrecked schooner after another. His heart sank as he came to realize he might be the lone survivor.

There were fifty-three of us. . . !

He passed the Lassiter wagon. Its bonnet and bow frames had been torn away, and huge chunks were missing from the sideboards. The twine they had tied to its wheel as a guideline was lying in a tangle on the ground. He ran past, only to be greeted by the wreckage of another wagon.

And then he reached his own.

It was intact. Fully. Untouched.

"Lisabeth!" He climbed up the back and peered inside.

No one was there.

He turned and looked out over the meadow, into the darkness, shouting Lisabeth's name again and again before finally giving up and climbing into the wagon.

Hanging a lantern on a convenient hook, he lay on his back and wrapped himself in a heavy blanket, catching his breath as he tried to conceive a plan of action. The only sounds were those of his own breathing, his own heartbeat.

"Does *Chayatocha* have her?" he whispered.

Or Michael? Or any of them? Have they already been killed? Are they lying out there in the dark—?

The image of Jeb's skull filled his mind.

—or in the thing's cave?

Realizing that madness might follow if he indulged that line of thought, he shook his head violently, telling himself repeatedly that such a fate had not befallen his loved ones.

"There's *got* to be a way to kill that thing. . . ."

He sat up, shoved a few loose items aside, and dug through one of his trunks.

Where is it? I know it's here. . . .

He pulled one book after another from the chest and tossed it aside as the search continued. Finally, he reached his texts on Indian lore, withdrew them, and leaned back. Choosing one at random, he flipped it open and checked the index.

"Chayatocha," he muttered. "How do you spell that? 'K-i-' probably. . ." He scanned the page. "Kickapoo. . .Kiowa. . ."

Nothing.

"Or, 'C-h-' maybe?"

Still nothing.

I don't even know what tribe the old man was from. . .what they were called. . . .

"And did you ask? Nooooooo. . ."

He continued searching, but found no specific references. None of the Northwest tribes of which it spoke matched with his location, or with the things he had seen in the village.

"Maybe under 'evil spirits' in general. . ."

Even as he read, he scolded himself. Here he was, an enlightened, modern man of the nineteenth century, resorting to the absurdity of Indian magic in order to confront a deadly situation. But the events of the past day had proven one thing, if nothing else—the scientific handle he thought he had on the world was—ultimately—not attached to anything.

In one day, every fundamental thing he had held as true had been turned on its head. There *were* things that could not be analyzed, or quantified, or proven in a scientific laboratory. Still, he knew what he had seen. His framework of reality required a quantum shift, an adjustment of monumental proportions.

But first things first.

He scanned the pages, searching for something—*anything*—that related to his circumstances. Nothing made itself apparent, but he went back and checked again and again, reading and comparing accounts of one superstition after another, of tribe after tribe.

The adrenaline that had been pumping through his system began to release its hold. He found himself reading the same paragraphs over and over again as his focus began to wane. He had been too long without sleep, and despite the graveness of his predicament, his body would take its due.

He dropped the book as he fell back onto the haphazardly piled quilts left by his wife on the Yankee bed. He never heard it hit the floor.

◉ ◉ ◉

Paradine awoke, startled by a sound, and sat bolt upright in the near darkness. The lantern, almost out of fuel, had gone dim, but it cast just enough light for him to check his pocket watch.

Seven hours. . .

Struggling to sharpen his senses, he was unsure whether he had heard the sound or merely dreamt it.

A moment later, it happened again.

Something was moving around outside, right next to his wagon, and breathing heavily. He heard the lid of the jockey box as it was raised, then lowered.

Searching for valuables. . . ?

There was a new sound, a peculiar scraping, like that of claws against wood.

No. . .please. . . !

He glanced around and, in a moment of panic, realized he had no rifle, no pistol, nothing.

Not that it would have helped.

Has the thing come for me, as it threatened? Did I sleep through its call?

Paradine remained still, holding his breath, hoping but doubting the thing would go away. He heard it make its way along the side of the wagon, toward the rear.

Where *he* was.

Another few moments, it would round the back, and nothing would stand between him and certain death.

Maybe it's time. How long can I keep running. . . ?

The breathing moved around the side of the wagon, and it was louder now. Paradine forced himself to look, to face his end.

He saw a pair of eyes glinting, reflecting what remained of the lamp's glow. He could not look away.

They stared back.

"Howdy," came a voice—a *human* voice. "Sorry if I scared ya."

Paradine released the breath he had been holding, and his body went limp.

"You really did," he admitted.

"Beg your pardon. . .didn't mean nothin' by it."

Still quivering, the schoolteacher reached out and took hold of a second lantern. After shaking it to feel its whale oil slosh, he lit it using the last ghostly flicker of the first lamp.

The flame flared brightly, illumining the gaunt face of the visitor.

The man was ungroomed, his chestnut beard full and wide. He wore what looked like a beaver hat and a coat of buckskin lined with more fur. In his hands was a long rifle. He looked like every picture of a frontiersman Paradine had seen.

"What are you doing out there?" Paradine asked, nodding toward the jockey box.

"Lookin' for food," the man confessed. "You tend to find it in the strangest places. . .the way folks squirrel it away and all."

"Come on in," the teacher said. "I'll get you something."

The man climbed into the back of the wagon, set his long rifle down, and took a seat among the quilts.

"Ain't as cold as it was," he commented. "Goes up and down a bit, but never really thaws too much. But at least there's no wind. Not usually, anyway."

Paradine dug into the wooden chest that held his family's supply of dried foods. "I've got some jerky here. . .and dried apples. Not much, but you're welcome to it."

Pulling a tin plate out of storage, he served the stranger a generous portion. He found his water bottle shoved into the space between two crates. Fortunately, its contents were still liquid.

"Ice water," he said, pouring some into a metal cup and handing it to the man. "I wish I could offer you a nice hot cup of coffee, but—"

"This'll do nicely, friend." The man winked. "Much obliged."

"Daniel Paradine," the teacher said, extending a hand. "Bloom Township, Ohio."

The frontiersman took his hand firmly. "Call me Lucky. Pleased to meet'ya."

Paradine smiled. "You *must* be lucky, to still be alive in *this* place." He brightened a bit. "Have you seen a woman, about five and a half feet, light brown hair, in a blue-and-white dress? Or a boy about eight years old in a white shirt? Maybe wandering around and lost?"

"Can't say that I have," the frontiersman said. "This is a pretty

Lone Star #5115

1940 Power Plant Pkwy
Hampton, Virginia 757-262-9013

day, August 22, 2008 1:38:53 PM

Holder: BROTHERS/IVY
Type: VISA
Number: XXXXXXXXXXX7052
code: 011298

nt: $0.00

2.00
868

ree to pay above total amount
ding to cardissuer agreement
chant agreement if credit voucher

CUSTOMER COPY ***

big place, and this kind of dark makes it that much bigger."

"Oh," Paradine said. "Well. . ."

"A fella could wander around out there for weeks and never bump into the same thing twice."

"When you came here, was it with a wagon train?"

"Nope. Came in over the mountain one night. Next mornin', the sun didn't come up. Ain't seen it since."

"How long ago was that?"

"Hard to say," the man replied, swallowing a bite. "I reckon it's been a few months now, but I couldn't swear to it."

"We just got here yesterday. . .or the day before. I'm not sure anymore myself."

"Happens in these parts. Never personally owned a watch, and without the sun up there, it makes it kinda tough to keep track."

"Well, I've got a watch, and I'm *still* having trouble."

"Where were you headed?" Lucky asked.

"Willamette Valley, via the Oregon Trail."

"Beautiful country out that way. What steered ya in here?"

"Our scout told us there was an Indian attack ahead, so we diverted and left the trail in an attempt to bypass them."

"No Indians anywhere near the trail," Lucky said. "Not past Fort Hall. Not for a good while."

"I think we know that now. The thing that lives here. . .it affected Johnny's mind somehow. Made him lead us into a trap."

"Your people. . .are any of them still alive, that you know of?"

"I'm not sure," Paradine confessed. "A few died almost immediately. The thing tore up our wagons, took our livestock. The people I asked about before, my wife and son. . .they were alive the last time I saw them, but that was yesterday. My boy. . . Michael. . .he wandered off, and I'm scared to death something's happened to him."

"Got a good friend by that name," the frontiersman said. "Back home, up north a ways. . .but I ain't seen him in a good while. Was hopin' maybe ol' Mike could come down here and join up with me, that we could start an outpost and get the word out. But we all have a special callin', and I reckon his lies elsewhere. Wasn't meant to be."

Paradine barely heard him, his mind on his own family. "My wife, Lisabeth, vanished when everyone else did, while I was up in the cave. I came back, and—"

"Cave?" Lucky asked. "What cave would that be?"

"The beast. . .the monster that's doing all this. . .keeping us here. . .it lives up there. In a cave in the side of the mountain."

The man looked at him more intently. "You mean the monster that's been killin' everyone off?"

"According to the tribe that used to live in this valley, it's an evil spirit. I never would have believed that in a million years, but given everything that's happened, I don't have a better explanation. Not yet anyway, though I'm sure there *has* to be one. Something rational. Anyway, they call it *Chayatocha*. . .means 'devourer of the world' or something like that."

"What Indians would those be?" the man asked.

"Don't know the name of the tribe, but their village lies on the other side of the forest. Actually, there's only one left. . .an old man. Been trapped here since he was a little boy."

The man set his food aside, his face grim. "I seen it, ya know. Dark as night and big as a mountain. There was a party of settlers, drawn in here like yours was. The thing set upon 'em. . .I watched it take a man and an ox apart like they was paper. One of the most horrible things I ever seen, my whole life."

"When was that?"

"Not long after I got here."

Paradine nodded to one side. "There are a bunch of graves over there."

"Some are theirs," Lucky said. "But a lot of them folks just. . . *vanished.*"

"I think I know where they wound up," Paradine groaned, remembering the piles of bone he had seen. He would not allow himself to consider that his own family might have met the same fate.

He changed the subject. "You didn't happen to write an entry in someone's journal, did you? Found one in a chest out there."

"Me? Nawww," the frontiersman replied, with seeming embarrassment. "Truth be told, I don't. . .tend to write much."

"Oh," said Paradine. "I'm sorry. . .I didn't mean to—"

"Don't give it another thought," Lucky said, handing back the now-empty plate. He pushed his rifle aside and reclined a bit.

"You say you saw the thing close up?" Paradine asked. "Saw it killing a man?"

"Yup."

"How did you get away? For that matter, how did you manage to survive all this time?"

"I found some wagons over yonder a piece," he pointed. "Tore up pretty good. Guess they was here before that other party arrived. I crawled underneath there and just stayed a good while. Fact I *still* live under 'em, sleep under 'em. Not the most comfortable place in the world, but I'm used to that. Learned to find my way around well enough in the dark. . .always did have a good sense of direction."

"That's amazing," Paradine said, looking on in awe. "So, for months you've stayed alive by finding food in abandoned wagons?"

"Sometimes you come across a dead horse or ox or somethin'. Carcass don't go bad in cold like this. Sharp knife's all it takes, and a little perseverance."

"You eat it *raw?*"

"A man'll do all kinds of things to survive. Amazing what you can do when you have to."

Paradine drank from his water bottle, recalling the many sips he had given his wife and son.

"Do you think there's any way out of here?" he asked, fearing the answer. "Think maybe we could go back out over the mountain, the way you came in?"

"No," the frontiersman said. "Had to come over pretty high up. . .snows were just settin' in. By now, the passes are gone altogether. You'd never make it." He downed a gulp of water and bit into a piece of apple. "You said you went up there? Where it lives?"

"Yes."

"Well, don't misunderstand me, but why ain't ya dead?"

Paradine leaned back, mulling the question. "It wants me alive. . .for now. Says it wants to show me something tonight."

"It *talked* to ya?"

"Yeah," the teacher said. "It's not just an animal. . .it's more than that. Seems to have a brilliant mind, actually, but I can't begin to explain it."

"You got out with your whole skin, and you're going back up there?"

"I have to. It'll kill my family if I don't."

"You're a brave man," Lucky said, "facing somethin' like that more'n once. The Injun said it was an evil spirit?"

"Yes, but it sure *seems* solid enough. Though, with some of the things it's done—"

"Well," the haggard man said, "if there's one thing I do know, it's that there's a lot more to life than what a man can see. There's a whole spiritual world behind it all, where things move and come and go that men can't begin to fathom."

"That's pretty profound," the teacher said.

"I've been a lot of places, Mr. Paradine. Seen a lot of things. Met a lot of people. And a lot of what I found just don't fit in the box."

Paradine suddenly felt uneasy. He looked over his shoulder, toward the front of the wagon.

"You'd better go," he said, realizing his mistake. "I've been so stupid. It knows me, and where I am. If you've managed to stay hidden from it this long, I don't want it finding you on my account. It's dangerous for you to be here." He reached down and pulled free a cloth sack of hardtack and soda bread. "Take this."

The frontiersman, touched by the gesture, reached out a hand and accepted it.

"I won't forget this, Mr. Paradine," he said. They shook hands once more, and the man climbed out.

"Listen," said Lucky, "when you go back up to that cave, you watch yourself. You hear me?"

"I will."

"Don't you be worryin' about your wife and your boy—"

"If you find them," Paradine interrupted, "*hide* them. Please. And, soon as you can, get them out of here. Away from this valley, away from that *thing*. And there was another man, John Forrester. I don't know where he is now, but. . ."

"I'll keep an eye out."

He winked, turned, and vanished without a sound into the darkness.

The hours passed in silence, the stillness broken only by the turning of pages.

Paradine pored over his Indian texts, searching for anything that might be useful. Science had nothing to offer—not in a situation like this. The supernatural had become a grim reality. All the rules had changed.

With great reluctance, he considered the other options before him.

He had found no direct reference to the name *Chayatocha*, but an extended chapter on medicine men and their rituals showed some promise, given his new context.

Never in a million years would I have thought—

He reread one passage. Then again.

And again.

He dared a slight smile, but it was short lived.

Suddenly, a pressure engulfed him. Cold descended. Within his mind, seemingly echoing all around him, he heard a voice.

Come to us.

Chapter 10

You are late, Daniel Paradine.

"You called," the man said defiantly. "I came."

It sat for a moment on its grotesque throne, studying the schoolteacher, who remained near the entry to the chamber. Paradine felt increasingly uncomfortable as the creature scrutinized him—it was as if something were burrowing into his mind, creating in its wake a subtle and momentary swirl of frustration, as if he were struggling to recall an obscure memory.

Yet he was not.

"So you have," the creature nodded.

Paradine glanced around. The chamber had not changed, save the addition of a few dismembered horse and ox skeletons he did not recall seeing before. The air in the place was still heavy and cold and carried a sulfurous stench.

"It is a great gift we give you," Chayatocha stated, its guttural, plural voice a horror. *"Shall we begin?"*

"First," Paradine said, "I have something for you."

"Do you?" it asked, laughing at the absurdity of the statement.

He set his lantern on the floor, reached into his coat, and pulled free a small deerskin bag. Quickly, he sprinkled a line of ash across the floor at the mouth of the entry tunnel. Then, continuing almost the same motion, he poured a circle onto the floor, surrounding himself.

"What is this?" the thing demanded.

The ash depleted, Paradine dropped the bag to the ground. Moving quickly, he reached under his coat and withdrew a medicine bundle of wolf hide, decorated with feathers and bone. From it he took a small rattle and a wood-handled talisman, which bore at its tip the likeness of an eagle's head. Around his neck hung an amulet suspended on a leather cord—a circle of quartz surrounded by bone, the sacred "eye" of the Welakiutl medicine man.

"Stop!" Chayatocha commanded.

Knowing the attempt was a long shot at best, Paradine began to shake the rattle in one hand while holding the talisman high in the other. Words issued from his lips, words he had learned from Seukani during his brief detour to the old man's house and had memorized during his walk toward the cave.

"So-tu-lac-ti, kem-ja-wel-cha-na. . ."

"STOP!" the being shouted again.

Paradine closed his eyes, his heart pounding, and went on, hoping the protective ring of ash would do its job.

"Ka-na-su-lo-ta-ka, el-na-see-kee-tow! Brothers of the eagle, brothers of the bear. . ."

"We command you to stop!"

". . .I call upon you to come forth, to break free of your captivity and take vengeance upon Chayatocha, he who took from you your lives, your land, and your legacy. . ."

The air in the cavern began to move. The rattle continued to sound.

The thing leapt to its feet and bellowed in anger, its roar shaking the walls of the cave. It clutched its sides as if in pain, encouraging a terrified Paradine to continue.

"Take back that which is yours. . .carry this evil from your land! Banish him to the dark places beyond the world, the places where the water does not flow and the deer do not run, where the sun knows not the sky and the clouds bear no rain. . ."

A wind began to build in the chamber, chilling him.

"WE ORDER YOU!" it screamed. *"STOP OR YOU WILL DIE!"*

Paradine did not stop. His own life no longer mattered to him. All he could think of were his wife and son.

"Rise up," called the self-taught medicine man from Bloom Township, Ohio. "Rise up, and take your revenge! Free yourselves. . .know the rest of eternity as unbound spirits, hunting amid the herds of the heavenly places!"

A full gale filled the cavern, roaring and whistling against the walls. Paradine, careful to remain within the protective circle of ash, heard another sound amid the rushing winds. The distinctive clatter of bone against bone.

To his utter amazement, all around him the bone piles began to give up their dead. The display was horrifying, yet he could not look away as bones pulled themselves free of the places they had been discarded and came together.

Reassembling themselves, before his eyes.

"NO!" the thing roared at the center of the whirlwind, its amber eyes ablaze. *"YOU CANNOT DEFEAT US! WE ARE CHAYATOCHA!"*

In moments, dozens of full skeletons stood surrounding the beast, crouching as if ready to attack. Paradine, transfixed by the sight, did not hear the repeated clack of bone against ice as the two mummified bodies that for decades had stood sentry outside came rushing up the tunnel behind him. They brushed against him as they passed, paying him no attention, focused on joining their brothers in the center of the chamber.

And then, the battle began.

Paradine struggled to keep his feet as the skeletal combatants descended upon Chayatocha, covering him like warrior ants swarming upon much larger prey. The clatter of bones and the roar of the storm merged with the creature's deafening cries, forcing Paradine's hands over his ears. He dropped to his knees and huddled there, barely able to see in the midst of the maelstrom.

"NOOOOOOOOO!" sounded a final scream.

The winds faded. The roar ceased.

The cavern went still.

Chayatocha was gone, as were the skeletons of Seukani's tribal brothers.

The room became a little warmer.

Paradine fell back against the wall, drained and still shaking from the adrenaline pumping through his veins. For many long minutes he sat, replaying the incredible scene in his mind, knowing he had witnessed the impossible.

And not only had he witnessed the exorcism, he had *performed* it.

"I can't believe it," he repeated, awed and thrilled. "It worked. . .but it *couldn't* have. . . ." His analytical mind, tempered and disciplined through many years of dedicated study, could not fully allow for what he had seen.

"But then," he conceded, "if you can have a monster in the first place, and a valley of eternal night, what's a little vengeance from beyond the grave?"

He rose to his feet, took up his lantern, and headed down the tunnel. As he exited the mountainside, he became fearful.

It still was dark outside.

"How—?"

He pulled out his pocket watch.

Eleven thirty-three.

He breathed a sigh of relief.

Of course it's dark. It's the middle of the night.

Allowing himself a moment, he sat back against a boulder and laughed out loud. He felt a gentle breeze against his cheek. It tossed his hair slightly.

It was the first time he had felt that since entering the valley.

Weary, he knew he had to get back to the wagons, to try to find Lisabeth, Michael, and the surviving remnant of his party. Nothing could stop them from leaving, not now.

"I've got to find Lucky," he said out loud. "He'll help me, and together we'll find the others."

Paradine made his way down the mountain, excitement jumping within him, joy filling his heart.

I did it! I actually did it!

Carried on wings of joy, he ran through the dense firs that stood at the base of the mountain and out across the former hunting fields of the Welakiutl. It all was so familiar to him now—the forests, the fields, the frozen lake at the valley's center, and the village that lay on the opposite shore.

He passed the totems, slapping each in triumph as he ran past.

Be free, everyone! He smiled, thinking of the tortured souls of those who had carved the monuments. *Your time of captivity is over!*

Bounding up to Seukani's house, he paused at the entrance just long enough to knock, and entered. The elderly Indian rose from his place of meditation and hobbled forward in anticipation.

"You still live." He smiled, surprised and overjoyed.

"It worked!" Paradine said, barely able to believe it. "It was incredible."

"The life spirits truly have blessed you," Seukani said. "They called you into this place. It was you they chose to defeat the evil one."

"Here," Paradine said, setting his lantern aside. He reached up to pull away the necklace he wore.

"No," Seukani said, stopping him with a gentle hand. "That is yours now, as are the other things. The ritual came to you. . .I never knew of it. The spirits have chosen you, speaking to you through the writings of your people. Honor them by accepting these things as your own."

Paradine smiled, then reached out and embraced the old man.

"We'll be leaving soon," he said. "There's nothing to stop us now. I want you to come with us."

"Never have I left this place," said the man. "Never have I walked beyond the mountains. This is my home."

"You can't stay here by yourself," Paradine insisted. "Please. . . reconsider. Perhaps the spirits wanted you here only to help banish Chayatocha, and now you are to live out the rest of your days among friends."

Seukani looked around, still seeing his mother, his father, his family, his tribe in every wall, every corner, every knothole of the house.

"I will consider it," he said, but his tone was not a positive one.

Paradine placed the medicine bundle and its contents atop a wooden crate near the door. "Keep these for me. I'll be back for them."

"I will, my friend."

Paradine nodded a good-bye, then took his lamp and struck out toward the camp. Back through the woods, across the pastureland. More than once, he looked upward, hoping to see the stars, but they remained hidden by the overcast.

The darkness was not as thick as before. Nor was it as cold.

"Lucky!" he cried out, as he approached the old, abandoned wagons he and Forrester earlier had explored. "Can you hear me? It's Daniel Paradine. . . . It's okay now. . . ."

No answer came.

He pressed onward, past the graveyard, toward his own wagons and—he hoped—his family.

Soon, the crushed Lassiter wagon appeared out of the gloom. He climbed past its wrecked tongue and into the camp, then cut to the right.

"Lisabeth!" he called out, rounding toward his own schooner.

There came a response out of the darkness.

But not the one he wanted.

"You would do that to us?" thundered the voice of Death.

Paradine, now close enough to see, stopped cold.

The yellow eyes peered down.

Chayatocha loomed angrily before him, standing beside the wagon and as tall as its bonnet. Held high in its left hand was—

"No—!"

A woman in a white-and-blue dress hung lifelessly, her head and neck buried in the dark being's icy, crushing grip.

"You fool!" the creature said. *"Do you really think anything you can conceive of can destroy us? We walk as a god!"*

"Put her down!" Paradine demanded.

The air crackled with frost as the beast's eyes glowed more brightly. It shook the bloody corpse of the woman, which dangled and danced like a rag doll.

"Please," the man begged.

The creature laughed, then reached up with its other hand and brutally dug its claws into the limp form, tearing it open, ripping it apart.

"NO!"

Paradine rushed forward in a blind rage. Chayatocha hurled the woman hard against the side of the wagon, then backhanded the man, knocking him to the frozen ground.

"You think us so stupid as to just stand there," it rumbled, *"as you perform a true exorcism ritual? Have you so little respect for us, after all you have witnessed?"*

"I took a chance," Paradine said, cradling the elbow on which he had landed. It throbbed with pain.

"We should kill you here and now!"

"Do it, then!" Paradine shouted, looking toward the motionless form near him. "I'm tired of you and your games! Just get it over with!"

Chayatocha bent over him. *"We are far from finished with you, little man."*

Paradine turned aside, toward the tangle of white, blue, and crimson that lay beneath the wagon.

Lisabeth. . .

Weeping freely, he slumped to the ground and crawled to the woman's side.

"Oh, look," Chayatocha said in derision. *"He loves her. . . ."*

Reaching out, the tortured man tenderly turned her face toward his own.

At once, both horror and hope filled his heart.

Judith Lassiter. . . ?

The beast roared with laughter, enjoying Paradine's shocked expression. The man looked away from the body, finding a moment of shameful relief in the death of the woman, knowing it meant there remained a chance for Lisabeth.

"We never said it was your wife," it chortled. *"But we* will *find her, and when we do. . ."*

Paradine looked into the eyes of his tormenter.

She's still out there!

"What happened?" he asked the thing, changing the subject immediately. "The ritual. . .I *saw* it work. The skeletons got up and—"

"Got up and what?" the creature laughed, *"Like this?"* At once, Judith's body sprang to its feet and lifted its fists against the creature. It pounded away for a few moments, then crumpled into a heap, eyes open and unseeing.

Paradine realized he had been had.

"You? You did all that? All the bones, and the wind, and—?"

"Mere puppetry."

"But, *why* didn't it work? I knew your name. . .I'd memorized all the words. . ."

It laughed, long and loud. The sound chilled Paradine to the core.

"Perhaps you are not as intelligent as we had thought. Perhaps you are not deserving of the gift we would give you."

Paradine waited silently, expecting to die.

"No," it decided. *"We will not deprive you of our greatness. You shall bear witness to the fullness of our power. You will know the glory of our being."*

"I can't stop you," Paradine said with a dry mouth. He feared the worst.

"Let it be so."

There came a tornadic rush of wind. Paradine felt himself being lifted into the air, yet nothing touched him. A numbness overcame him as he was swept along through the darkness at great speed. It was hard to breathe. The arctic winds bit at his face and his hands. His senses swam.

Moments later, he was back in the cavern. The thing once again rested on its throne.

"Come closer."

The scholar blew on his hands to warm them, then took a fearful step forward. Then another. The being did not move, did not blink, its yellow eyes boring through Paradine's, their gazes locked.

"Stop there," it commanded, as the man drew to within a few feet. *"Set down your lantern."*

Paradine was amazed to realize that he still clutched the lantern. Without breaking eye contact, he bent down just enough to place it on the floor, and no sooner had it left his grasp than he felt a shift in the world around him. The odd light in the cavern went blue. Despite his dizziness, he did not move, did not fall. Rather, it was the world that fell away, replaced in the same swirling instant by another.

The light stung his eyes. He was outside somewhere. The sun was shining. Birds were singing. The sounds of life encompassed him.

"What. . . ? *Where. . . ?*"

"Welcome," came a voice, resonant yet not threatening.

Paradine looked up into a face, that of a mountain of a man. Rugged, even handsome, the face bore a square jaw and sculpted features. The man's eyes were blue and piercing, his hair dark and long. He wore a bronze helmet studded with silver on his head. His breastplate glittered in the sun—interlocking plates of dark metal lined with gold. Bronze shin guards covered his lower legs, and he wore heavy, segmented sandals on his feet. The massive sword on his belt, crafted of prismatic metals and covered with an intricate inset pattern, sparkled as it protruded from its sheath. In his left hand was an elongated shield, which bore the insignia of the kingdom he served.

The teacher whirled to find himself on a city street like none he had seen. Great structures of brick and asphalt rose on all sides, complex buildings born of exquisite architectural science. Many were incomplete, as if the entire metropolis were being built at once. Even unfinished, they towered into the air, well suiting the mammoth size of the people moving fluidly along the street.

Though Paradine was nearly six feet tall, everyone on the street dwarfed him. He felt like a child among adults. The huge soldier before him was not an aberration here, but a man of common size.

"Who are you?"

"I am your host," the colossus intoned, bowing.

"But, *how. . . ?*"

"I am Gorgathuus, soldier of soldiers, serving in the army of the greatest king ever to live."

Paradine struggled for words. He was articulate and well read, but he had never considered a world like this.

"Where are we?" he managed.

"A place of wonder. Come."

Paradine knew he beheld the impossible, yet he chose to embrace the experience, to let it unfold before him. The soldier led him down the street, past dozens of people who clearly recognized Gorgathuus and paid their respects. No one took any notice of the tiny man at his side, however, nor did anyone bother to step out of his way.

"Everyone's so *big*," Paradine said nervously. "Why? Where is this?"

"All is as it was."

"That's not an answer."

I'm dreaming. I have to be.

The soldier, amused, patted him on the shoulder as they turned down a side street.

The pungent aroma of baking bread and roasted meat filled the air. Music played, of a type Paradine did not recognize, the sound coming from instruments unknown to him. Both laughter and cries of anger met his ears as they moved along.

Everywhere, he heard the buzz of speech. Citizens speaking to shopkeepers, mothers scolding children, overseers barking orders.

"Everything about this place seems *ancient*," Paradine said. "Yet they're all speaking contemporary English."

"They are not," Gorgathuus said.

"But I *understand* them. . .every word. . ."

"You understand them because *I* understand them. I am your *host*."

"That makes no sense."

The street widened. The crowds grew more dense.

"We are here," the soldier said, leading him into a vast courtyard, the majestic focal point of dozens of streets and walkways. Magnificent statues of men and beasts stood upon high pedestals, encompassing the square. A city center, filled with people, filled with life. The roar of voices was everywhere.

But for all its splendor, the bustling square was not the focus of Paradine's attention. Instead, his gaze was upward, to something that dominated the scene, less than a hundred yards away.

"Behold," said Gorgathuus.

The immense structure at the city's heart cast an inescapable shadow over the inhabitants' lives. Rising to a height of 650 feet, the pyramid, a triumph of human engineering, was a quarter-mile square at the base and so beautiful as to defy adequate description. Made of the same reddish brick as the surrounding buildings, it boasted vast, exquisite sculptures of marble on its many flowing tiers. Some sections appeared unfinished, while in other places waterfalls cascaded in designed patterns along the outer flanks, creating a white, subtle roar. Lush plant life blossomed in the many climbing gardens that graced the lower levels, bringing a sense of vitality as they lined the zig-zagging stairways leading to a flattened pinnacle.

Atop the summit rose an ornate temple, on which stood an enormous statue of a man dressed as a hunter.

"Glorious, is it not?" said an awed Gorgathuus. "It is nearly complete. . . ."

"Where exactly are we?" Paradine asked again.

"My home."

A trumpet blast filled the air, echoing from seemingly

everywhere. A door opened in the soaring temple, and onto a wide, sculpted balcony there emerged a man and a woman, both draped in regal robes and headgear of glittering gold. At that distance, Paradine could not discern their faces.

But those around him knew exactly who the couple was.

The man raised his arms. Everyone immediately dropped to their knees and lowered their heads, even those out of sight of the tower, who seemingly took their cue from those in the square. Tens of thousands of people, moving as one, all bowing to their king and queen. A chant arose, voiced in unison by everyone.

Almost everyone.

Paradine, still standing, saw a group of seven people standing some distance away who refused to kneel or otherwise pay homage. A group of soldiers dressed in the same manner as Gorgathuus rushed toward them. Defiantly, the protesters stood their ground, unyielding and unafraid—right up until the moment when broad, flashing swords separated their heads from their shoulders.

Nearer by, Paradine saw three others also standing rebelliously, knowing the act would cost them their lives. He became aware that Gorgathuus had lunged forward, sword drawn.

The gleaming blade came down. Once, twice, thrice.

Paradine, horrified, watched as his host casually returned to his side, pausing along the way to wipe his sword against the back of a kneeling man, bloodying his white robes.

"On your knees!" Gorgathuus ordered his guest, even as he himself dropped to the ground in worship. Paradine quickly knelt, finding the sunbaked street beneath him warm and smooth.

Again, he lifted his eyes to the balcony above, squinting in the bright light of day. No one else dared lift their eyes. After a moment, the king and queen turned and disappeared back through the portal. The trumpet again sounded. Everyone in the city looked up, rose, and the day's activities resumed.

The soldier and the schoolteacher moved along, down a side street and into another district. Paradine, certain now that he was in the midst of a dream, looked around in wonder, taking in the hanging works of art, the dancing, the songs. They paused for the performance of a street magician, listened to the pitch of a seller of child slaves, and watched as two men in a tiled pit, cheered by onlookers, fought to the death. Paradine was aghast at the lack of compassion he saw around him.

They walked on, and another mile fell behind them. Finally, they stopped before a large edifice where several large but beautiful dark-haired women stood in a doorway, almost writhing in anticipation. Their translucent clothing was far more revealing than anything Paradine had seen—he averted his eyes, struggling to think only of his wife's face.

"Oh, come now," Gorgathuus mocked. "As if such enticing visions of loveliness have not filled your mind, and repeatedly."

Paradine remained silent. At once, the women were upon the soldier, running their hands over and under his armor, caressing his face and arms, and standing on the tips of their toes in order to kiss him fully and passionately. They did not so much as look at Paradine, who maintained a modest distance.

"They missed me," the soldier said with an audible leer.

"Apparently so."

"I come here often."

One of the women spoke, her tone deeply seductive. Then another. All three women implored Gorgathuus to join them. Their words were vulgar, their intent clear. The massive warrior clearly loved feeling their soft hands on his flesh.

Too much so. He lingered for a moment too long, delighting in the sensuous whispers of his favorite, a full-lipped, raven-haired beauty.

In midsentence, her words fell away into gibberish.

Suddenly, everywhere, screams filled the air. A strange panic swelled in the streets, disintegrating in minutes to utter chaos. Fighting and rioting broke out as confusion reigned. The women hanging upon Gorgathuus tried to speak to him and to each other, but the words that spilled from their lips were not in the language they had shared a moment before.

In an instant, Paradine knew.

Babel!

He swung back toward the tower, still visible above the crowns of the surrounding buildings.

Nimrod and Semiramis!

"Yes," said the soldier from directly behind him. He knew Paradine's thoughts even amid the bedlam. "It is they. . .king and queen, god and goddess!"

Paradine remembered his texts. The husband and wife had ascended to godhood in the eyes of their people, building a religion around themselves that would mutate and evolve throughout the ages. It would form the basis of Baal and Ashtaroth worship, and would bring forth the gods and goddesses of Greece, Rome, Egypt, and many other lands—some of which were still worshiped in modern times.

But Babel existed thousands of years ago—

"Yes."

On the Tigris and Euphrates rivers.

"Not the originals, of course," Gorgathuus said. "Those

166

perished when the earth was so cruelly destroyed by water. . . ."

That forsaken thing sent me back in time!

"Did it, now?" grinned the soldier. "Impressed?"

"Stop it!" Paradine shouted, clutching his temples. "Get out of my head!"

The soldier angrily gripped the schoolteacher's throat, then leaned down into his face and squeezed.

"I will do as I wish," he threatened. *"My* life, *my* rules."

Paradine, his face reddening, nodded assent.

"Do not think you cannot *die* in here," Gorgathuus warned, releasing his grip.

In where?

Gorgathuus reached down with a huge hand and grabbed Paradine by the arm, almost yanking it out of its socket. The teacher felt his weight slip away, and no longer were his feet beneath him. Babel broke into a wave of disjoined fury, went silent, and was gone.

◎ ◎ ◎

The dizziness passed quickly, and Paradine found his feet on solid ground once more.

It was night, and wisps of gray smoke hung low in the air. The full moon shone down, huge and silver, from amid a sky of bright stars. The light of a thousand torches burned on the horizon, where a vast expanse of white stone structures stood, mottled with dark, moving things. Screams arose, lessened by the distance but nonetheless chilling.

A city under siege.

The hilly countryside could have been anywhere, anytime.

Around him, the ground was littered with—

No!

He spun, realizing that he stood in the middle of a vast battle-field. Overturned chariots and wagons burned far and wide, casting orange light and thick smoke into the cool night air, stinging his eyes, burning his throat. Broken swords, pierced shields, and splintered spears cluttered the landscape for as far as he could see. Everywhere were the dead and dying, many thousands maimed and wounded beyond the ability to survive. Voices of agony cried out—moans and cries, the last gasps of violent lives nearing end. The soil, soaked with blood, was sticky against the soles of his boots.

One voice, weak but familiar, sounded at his feet.

"Paradine," it whispered.

He looked down. Gorgathuus lay on his back, the life streaming profusely from his mouth, nose, and eyes. His left arm and both legs were badly broken, twisted into horrendous positions. The giant warrior stared as if unable to see.

Paradine bent down, listening.

"I'm here," he said.

"This is the moment," Gorgathuus said, choking on blood.

"What moment?"

A light caught Paradine's eye. He looked up and saw—in the distance but closing—a small and yellowish light, hovering low over the carnage as if cast by a source above, yet no source was apparent. It moved here and there, curving in its course, casting its glow upon the corpses and near-corpses as it passed.

"What moment?" the scholar repeated.

"My birth," the soldier said, his voice fading.

The light approached, crossing the final distance. Paradine stepped back, fearful of the odd radiance. It paused over

Gorgathuus as if hanging in the air, bathing his breastplate. Its presence revealed to Paradine just how severely wounded the man was—not only had he sustained the injuries evident in his arm and his legs, but his body armor had been pierced through, laying him open across the midsection, exposing internal organs that glistened wetly.

"*Yes,*" Gorgathuus whispered unevenly, as if in answer.

The light remained motionless for another moment. Paradine watched as the soldier drew deeply and erratically of the battle-scarred air, taking what was surely his final breath.

Suddenly, the light plunged through the man's armor and into his body. Paradine, disbelieving, saw a light appear behind the man's eyes. It filled his body, tracing along his arms, his legs.

Another light rushed toward them, across the bloody landscape. Then another. And another. A wind picked up out of nowhere. It grew cold. Paradine stood back as each shining orb in turn slammed into the wounded soldier without hesitation.

They came too quickly. Paradine lost count at more than a hundred.

Gorgathuus shuddered, his teeth clenched in pain, his fists trembling, his eyes squeezed tightly shut. He cried out as his body tensed, his arms and legs becoming straight and stiff. His spilled blood seemed to reverse its flow, seeping back into the copious wounds from which it had come, before the wounds themselves began to close.

And then, it was over. The cold vanished. The air went still.

Paradine looked down at the man. Where once a gaping abdominal injury had been, he saw only healthy flesh. The mangled legs and arm were twisted no more.

Gorgathuus began to breathe freely. He opened his eyes,

looked into the night sky, then up at Paradine.

"The first moment," he said, a hint of triumph in his strengthening voice.

"I don't understand," said the teacher.

"You will."

Without assistance, the soldier rose to his feet, held his arms wide, and shook his fist at the heavens.

"I live!" he cried out, defiantly and victoriously. *"I live!* You thought to destroy me, yet failed!"

Paradine, still backing away, tripped over a dismembered corpse and fell hard to the ground. Gorgathuus laughed, walked up to the man, and pulled him to his feet with ease.

"What is all this?" the teacher managed, overwhelmed.

The warrior threw his head back and roared in triumph. Putting a huge hand around Paradine's shoulders, he pulled him close and bent down to recover his massive, red-stained sword from where it lay.

The world swirled away around them.

Paradine found himself back in the cave, standing as if he had not moved and staring still at his monstrous keeper. For an instant his equilibrium was off, forcing him to catch himself with a step forward to avoid falling.

Chayatocha sat regally, spread upon his ghastly throne.

"You saw the great soldier?" it asked, the voice an anguished sea.

"I did."

"You saw the world as it once was? The glory of battle?"

"Yes. . .and no."

The creature nodded.

"You do not yet appreciate our gift. You have much yet to witness."

The being's tone of voice struck Paradine as anomalous, almost maudlin. As he watched, it closed its eyes.

"*But not this night,*" it went on. "*Leave. We will summon you again when it is time.*"

Paradine stepped back, pausing to retrieve his lantern from the floor. Its light illumined the mound of treasure across the chamber.

His eyes fell upon one silvery object, protruding upright from the glittering mass.

The sword of Gorgathuus!

"*Yes,*" Chayatocha said, rising from the bone pile. "*Now, go.*"

"Where?"

"*It matters not. We will call for you when the hour arrives. Do not disappoint us.*"

The man turned and headed down the tunnel. Behind him, he heard the metal-on-metal slide of a blade pulling free. Fighting the urge to return for a look, he stepped out into the darkness.

He checked his watch and stared in disbelief at its pearly face.

More than five hours had passed since the encounter at the camp.

Chapter 11

He was tired,
too tired to make the trip back to the wagons.

Paradine sat on a boulder only a short distance from the cave entrance, trying to assimilate all he had seen and heard and felt.

The darkness and the silence surrounded him. He struggled. It all was too much.

"I just want my family," he whispered to himself. "I just want to get out of this godforsaken valley, and get to Saraleah, and get our lives back."

A voice called out, low but distinctive.

"Daniel."

He turned downslope, straining to see into the inky blackness.

Holding his lantern up, he saw a shape emerging, coming into the light.

"Lucky!"

"Shhhhh," the frontiersman said, leaning against his rifle. "Not so loud. Come on down here, away from the mouth of that thing."

Paradine climbed downhill, meeting the man behind a large stone outcropping.

"What are you doing here?" he asked.

"I overheard that monster," Lucky said. "Back at your camp. Remembered what you said about the cave, and figured that was where you were headed. Stopped to bury that poor woman, then followed the cliffs on around. Finally saw the light of the cave."

"I guess you figured right."

"So, what's going on? What's it doing up there?"

"Have you found my family?"

"I wish I could say I had," replied the bearded man. "Awful lot of darkness out there to be lost in. And one can't go hollerin', not with that thing on the prowl."

"I know," Paradine said, disappointed.

"Come on. . .come with me. I'll hide you proper."

"I can't."

"Why not?"

"Because," Paradine began, his voice heavy, "I have to get back up there when the time comes."

"To the cave? That's crazy talk."

"You don't understand. It's wanting to show me things. . .giving me glimpses into the past. People, places. It's sending me back in time, somehow, and it isn't finished yet. I just hope it doesn't *strand* me there."

"Back in time? Don't seem possible."

Paradine shook his head, disappointed in himself for having so few answers. "I don't know. Maybe I dreamed the whole thing. I mean, really. . .*Babel?*"

"Babble? Daniel, I'm sorry, but I don't understand."

"I don't, either. All I know is, whatever it's doing, I'd better be here and ready whenever it calls."

"*Why*, for heaven's sake?"

"Every minute I'm with that thing is one minute it isn't out hunting for my family. If I could be in there right now, I would be, but it kicked me out for some reason. Told me to stay nearby, though. . .*ordered* me, is more like it. And it already told me that if I don't show up when it wants, it'll kill off everyone still alive in the valley, including my wife, my son, the old man, and you." He took a breath, thinking back. "It slipped up back at the camp. Let me know that Lisabeth's still alive. I'm hoping Michael is, too, and I want them to *stay* that way."

The frontiersman looked into Paradine's eyes, then up at the glowing cave entrance high above.

"Daniel Paradine," he said, "you are one brave man."

"No," the man said. "I just love my family. You're the brave one. It has a reason to keep me alive, but if it catches *you* out here, it'll kill you for sure."

"Ain't caught me yet."

"Still, I wouldn't push my luck." He dimmed the lantern a bit.

"What's it like?" Lucky asked. "Up close?"

"For one thing, it's got an ego as big as all outdoors. Can't understand why."

"What do you mean?"

"The thing always refers to itself in the plural, with the royal *we*. *We* did this, *we* did that, *we're* so great. . ."

175

"Maybe it's just gone loco."

"I hope not," Paradine sighed. "The only thing worse than a remorseless, murdering evil spirit is an *insane*, remorseless, murdering evil spirit." He looked off into the distance. "Remember that old man I told you about? Seukani?"

"The Injun? Sure."

"He said the thing is really old, and I believe it. For one thing, it would take a long time to get *that* ugly." He tossed a pebble. "But now you've got me thinking. . .can a being be around for that long and remain sane?"

"Hope so."

"Listen," Paradine said. "Seukani lives in a village just over there, on the other side of the frozen lake. Think you could find it?"

"Ain't been over that way, not yet. But I reckon I could."

"Row of wooden houses, totem poles out front."

"Easy enough."

"You mentioned having been up north. Speak any French?"

"Enough to get by," Lucky said.

"Good. So does he. Get over there and give him a warning. Tell him I sent you. Tell him the incantation didn't do anything after all. I don't know why, but it didn't." He rubbed his forehead. "Don't know why I ever thought it could work in the first place."

"What incantation?"

"He'll know. Tell him he'll need to keep on protecting himself until I can figure out something else."

"Protectin' hisself? How?"

"Long story. I wouldn't have believed it in a million years, and neither would you. . .but he's still here, so it must be true. Just warn him, all right? Don't hang around his place too long, though. I don't think it would be safe for you. You'll have to keep hiding wherever you've been hiding."

"All right, Daniel," the man agreed. "I'll do it."

"How'd you find your way up here in the dark, anyway?" Paradine asked, noting the man's lack of a lantern. "And come to think of it, you didn't have a light back at my wagon, either."

He smiled and winked. "Do most of my travelin' at night. These old eyes are used to darker places than this. Like a cat's. You should see the forests of Quebec at midnight. Black as pitch."

"Well, be careful. If you do need a lantern, take one from my wagon. You'll find oil there, too, in one of the barrels on the ground next to it."

"Thank you kindly," the man nodded. "Don't worry about me or your family."

"I'll try not to."

"You watch yourself, now. You hear me?"

"I will. You, too."

Lucky silently slipped away down the mountain, leaving Paradine alone with his tangled thoughts, his unanswered questions, his lingering hopes.

◉ ◉ ◉

Seukani sat up on the mat where he had been sleeping. Once again, the dreams had come, dreams of a time, a place, where he was not alone, where he was surrounded by souls too numerous to count.

Surrounded by love, and light, and joy.

They comforted him, as always, like a warm touch, a soothing voice. As he awoke more fully, he thanked his mother and father, for surely it was they who spoke to him through the dreams, helping him to know he was not alone.

In the dim light of the fire's dying embers, he rose to his feet, casting a gentle shadow upon the wall. Wrapping himself in a blanket, he made his way over to the door. It creaked as he slowly opened it and peered out into the stillness that always engulfed his village. He saw nothing.

Yet he knew that *something* was out there, moving within the darkness. He could feel it.

His gaze was immediately drawn toward the cave high on the mountain, where for so long the cause of his misery, his loneliness, had lived.

He sensed a presence still, sensed its power. He knew it still walked the valley—touching his mind, knowing his thoughts, his fears.

Surely it is morning by now, yet the sun has not returned to the sky.

Fearful once again, he closed the door.

◎ ◎ ◎

Come to us.

Paradine rose from the hard ground where he had been sleeping, wedged into the crag of a large, flattened boulder where he could find a modicum of warmth. His pleasant dream of home had ended abruptly with the call, which had pierced his subconscious and brought him immediately to full awareness.

"Give me a minute," he muttered.

He struggled to his feet, dusted himself off, and began the ascent. The route was becoming familiar to him—he might have been able to find his way back to the cavern even without the ominous amber glow.

Again he was met by the sulfurous scent, the heavy, wet chill.

He found Chayatocha again on its gruesome throne, contemplating a skull it held up before its face.

"Alas, poor Yorick," it said. *"I knew him, Horatio. A fellow of infinite jest. . ."*

"Quoting an inferior race?" Paradine asked.

"You have your moments."

"I'm here," the man said flatly.

In silence, the creature studied him.

"Come forward," it finally said, its voice bubbling up as if from a deep pit.

Paradine set the lamp on the ground as before. Again, he looked into the thing's horrible eyes.

"Again we will send you to the great warrior who serves the spirits," it said. *"Through him you will learn of our greatness."*

The light in the cavern went blue, and again Paradine found himself elsewhere.

This time, much to his disbelief, he knew where he was.

Concealing himself in the hollow of a high, arching doorway so as not to be trampled by the passing crowds, Paradine's eyes darted from side to side as he gathered his bearings. Everywhere, the writing, the artwork, the architecture screamed to him of a single place, a single people. Unlike the populace he had witnessed at Babel, the people around him now were of conventional height. But like before, no one seemed to take any notice of Paradine, even when nearly walking into him.

He lifted his eyes, and the sight nearly drove the breath from his lungs. Before him rose a colossal stone monument, an imposing figure carved directly into the limestone bedrock on which the city rested. Stretching more than two hundred feet in length and resting upon enormous haunches, its scarlet-crowned head rose more than sixty feet into the air. Its painted eyes stared forward, fixed upon the eastern horizon, unblinking and eternal.

Paradine never had seen the masterwork in its entirety, but there was no mistaking that massive head. He had seen it in photographs—almost buried by the shifting dunes and battered by centuries of windblown sands, the elements had worked to wipe it from existence. Yet still it remained.

The Sphinx!

The huge figure had not yet suffered the full ravages of time. It had aged, to be sure, its body weathered and fractured, reinforced here and there by casing stones. Its head, however, appeared almost pristine by comparison.

"A wonder, is it not?" asked a voice. "It is the very soul of Egypt."

Paradine turned and, to his surprise, found Gorgathuus standing behind him, concealed in the shadows of the entryway, within what Paradine now realized was an ornate temple. The towering man was clad not in the armor of a soldier, but in the colorful robes of Egyptian royalty.

"This grand monument did not always bear such a visage," the huge man continued. "Once, it was a great and noble lion, when it was first cut from the rock. For years, its builders worked, day and night. When finally they were finished, it was a masterpiece, polished to gleam in the light of the sun. But it was only stone. . .and once its makers vanished from this earth and could maintain it no longer, the rains and winds took their toll. All in all, it has held up well."

"How can *you* be here, in Giza?" Paradine demanded. "It must have been thousands of years since—"

"Giza? No, not yet. This is *Rosetau.*"

"Rosetau then. The point is, how—?"

"Are you not at all curious about this great work of man?"

Gorgathuus asked, looking up at the Sphinx. "Do you not wish to learn something about it that no other man knows?"

"All right, then," the scholar said. "What do you mean, 'it used to be a lion'?"

"The ancients, who lived during the First Time, long before the Egyptians came to this land. . .it was *they* who built it. For centuries it stood here, forgotten and alone, buried up to its neck by the sands."

"A lost civilization? But, it has a pharaoh's head—"

"Have you noticed how *small* the head is, compared to the body? These fine craftsmen chipped away at a roaring lion, and created the likeness of an invincible king."

"How do you know all this? How do you even know there *were* 'ancients'?"

Gorgathuus shook his head in amusement. "Do I really have to say it, Mr. Paradine?"

He took the teacher by the shoulder and led him to a slightly different vantage point. He directed Paradine's gaze toward a structure in the distance. Enclosed in ramped scaffolding and only half completed, its identity nonetheless was unmistakable.

"Behold. . .the crowning achievement of human history."

"The Great Pyramid," Paradine said, barely able to believe it.

Gorgathuus's intense pride surrounded him like a suffocating cloud. "It will last throughout the ages, to stand forever as mankind's greatest accomplishment."

"Very nice," the teacher said, reluctant to feed the man's ego.

Disappointed in Paradine's response, Gorgathuus guided him through a wide doorway and into the central chamber of the temple complex. The air was warm and dry, and sunlight filtered through an opening in the ceiling. A dozen armed guards dropped to their knees as the men entered, bowed their heads, and cast their eyes downward. Gorgathuus stood in their midst, surrounded by soaring walls filled with magnificent works of art, all portraying the military triumphs of a single man.

"My life," he said, surveying the murals, "in glorious color."

"All right," Paradine said, scrutinizing the display. "Assuming any of this is real in the first place, I want to know why you're still alive. I want to know how a man can live for thousands of years."

"You saw my rebirth on the battlefield, did you not?"

"I saw you healed."

"It was no mere healing. Moment by moment, day by day, I am sustained by many. No longer will I fall by the blade, or through pestilence, or by poison, or due to the passing years, or for any other cause you can name. I am made immortal. . .and through them, I will live forever."

"Through *whom?*"

"Through the old ones. I live through them, and they walk through *me.*"

"You speak in riddles."

"Do not blame your lack of comprehension on me, Mr. Paradine."

Paradine looked around the room, studying the kneeling men, who remained motionless, as if afraid even to breathe. Each was dressed identically in light armor, their heads shaven except for ponytails that hung from the backs of their heads. Each bore a spear some six feet in length, tipped with a head of glistening copper.

"So," Paradine asked, "who are you, that they're all down on their knees like that?"

Gorgathuus laughed. "They kneel because they value their lives. I am the only god they worship, the only god they know. The temples of such false gods as Ra and Horus and Osiris have been closed throughout the land, and will remain so."

Paradine backed toward the doorway.

It's impossible—!

He turned and looked once more at the great stone face of the Sphinx. With awakened eyes, he saw.

It was the image of Gorgathuus.

"Yes," the huge man gloated, satisfied at the spark of awe in Paradine's eyes. "Here, I am Khufu, ruler of Egypt, who ascended the throne upon the death of my adopted father, Sneferu, whose rule, sadly, was cut short."

"By you?" Paradine asked unevenly, overwhelmed by the scope of it all.

A familiar, wicked laugh echoed throughout the temple. It was the last thing Paradine heard before vertigo descended and the room was swept away from around him.

◎ ◎ ◎

The sun was gone. Light no longer flooded his eyes, but the warm flicker of torchlight glowed softly. The air was stale with the heavy musk of mildew and damp stone, rotting hay and death.

Paradine leaned into a rough-hewn pillar, gathering his wits and his balance. As far as he could tell, he was alone. Into the walls around him were set barred portals, openings into cells beyond. One held the remains of a prisoner, long dead and likely forgotten. Paradine searched for an exit, finally locating a wide staircase that led to unknown heights.

A dungeon.

At the center of the roughly circular chamber stood the massive base of an ancient grinding mill, connected to a wide shaft that disappeared through a hole in the ceiling. Heavy wooden beams protruded in a spoke-like fashion from a stone hub. A circular path had been worn into the floor by the many who had lived out their lives in that room, pulverizing grain for the use of their captors.

He heard a clanking of chains and realized the mill was slowly turning. Someone was behind it, out of sight for the moment, putting all of his strength into the effort.

That someone was the prison's only captive.

A figure emerged, shrouded in the gloom. Large and muscular, the man was shackled to the mill, visibly suffering with each step he took. His short, black hair was scraggly and unwashed. His clothes were rags, his feet bare. As he came around the mill, he seemingly took no notice of the nineteenth-century schoolteacher standing near him.

Paradine quickly understood why.

The man's eyes were gone, leaving dark, gaping cavities. Scars surrounded the holes, above and below. Crudely and cruelly, Paradine knew, a blade had taken them.

"Indeed," whispered a proud voice. "My own."

Paradine looked to his left and found Gorgathuus standing in the shadows, dressed once more in a warrior's armor. His breastplate and tunic were red. He wore a golden headband with inset gems of green and blue. His hair, once long and dark, was short-cropped and had gone white. His face showed deep fissures and other changes, but not as the lines that age would carve—they seemed more like the scars of pestilence.

"Gorgathuus," Paradine said, knowing him at once, despite the transformation. "Where is this? Egypt still?"

"Hardly," said the giant. "Much time has passed since I left that land. And here, I am known as Vordoc, slayer of the Hebrews."

"Not Khufu?" Paradine asked. "You of all people. . .why would you give up being a pharaoh?"

"I grew weary of it," the warrior confessed. "The throne bored me. I missed the action of combat. . .the thrill of war. . .the feel of my sword sliding into the flesh of another. So, after a few decades of worship by a people who never truly appreciated my brilliance, I feigned my death and went back to the life I love, that of a mercenary."

"How long ago was that?"

Gorgathuus smiled. "Does it matter?"

"Yes, it matters."

Paradine saw that no answer was forthcoming. "Well, forgive me, but I'm going to call you Gorgathuus. Just to keep it straight."

"If you must."

The captive at the mill stopped in his tracks, listening. "Who's there?"

"Back to work!" shouted Gorgathuus. "As long as you work, you live!"

The chained man leaned into the protruding beam and continued his labor. Gorgathuus led Paradine a short distance down a side corridor, away from the man at the millwheel.

"So, where is this?" Paradine asked again.

"Gaza," his host informed him.

Gaza? What people lived in Gaza?

"Look at that brute. He should consider himself lucky. . .his punishment should have been death."

"What did he do?"

"He murdered more than a thousand of my adopted people."

There's that word—adopted—again.

"And how many of *his* people have *you* killed?"

Gorgathuus laughed proudly. "Many more than that, I promise you."

Paradine watched the prisoner with increasing empathy, wishing he could free the man. *I know how you feel—being held captive.*

"So you blinded him?"

"Like a witless animal, he fell into a trap we set. I wanted to bury my dagger in his heart but was forbidden from doing so. He was the great defender of the Israelites, but no more. See how his God has forgotten him! Such a fool he was, serving that egocentric tyrant."

As Paradine stood pondering the man, a palace guard appeared on the stone stairway that led up from the prison, dressed in the same manner as Gorgathuus. Upon seeing his comrade-in-arms, the sentry paused and gestured for his attention.

Seeing to the need of the guard, Gorgathuus left Paradine's side. The teacher stepped forward and neared the suffering man, halting several feet short of the swing of his shackled arms, just in case.

"Is there anything I can do?" he asked. "Do you need water?"

No reply.

"Who are you?" Paradine went on. "Please. . .I'm not one of those who imprisoned you here. I want to help."

Nothing. No reaction at all.

Puzzled, Paradine stepped back. The young guard who had descended the stairs moved toward the prisoner, a drawn dagger in his hand.

"Leave him alone," Paradine warned, but the guard showed no sign of having heard him. "Hey," he tried again, moving to block the man's way. "What do you think you're—?"

Paradine was yanked back firmly by Gorgathuus.

"Stay out of matters that do not concern you."

"What's happening? What's he doing?"

"The lords have requested that the prisoner be brought upstairs. They are holding a banquet in honor of the god Dagon, and wish for their thousands of guests to be entertained by this criminal's presence."

The guard pulled heavy iron pins from the chains holding the man to the mill, freeing him. The prisoner fell to his knees.

"Get up," ordered the guard, who was much smaller than the captive. The sightless man rose to his feet, staggering, and allowed himself to be led across the room and up the stairs.

Paradine worked to piece it all together as the beleaguered man disappeared from sight.

Gaza. What was it about Gaza?

Within his memory, a few stubborn clues began to trickle free. Gorgathuus watched him. Heard him.

A blinded man. . .

And then, he remembered.

"Samson!"

"Indeed," laughed Gorgathuus.

"The Philistines! You're fighting for the Philistines? Why?"

"I go where I am paid."

"You know what's going to happen up there," Paradine said. "You must. Any time now—"

"I do not foretell the future."

"Yes, you do. On that battlefield, when you were dying. . .you knew that whatever-it-was was coming to heal you. And you recognized the name *Giza* when I mentioned it."

"I do not know the future," Gorgathuus insisted. "I remember the *past.*"

What?

Paradine, working to reason it out, moved to the base of the curving stairway and stood peering upward.

"What's *that* supposed to mean?" he demanded, his frustration apparent. "And why am I being shown these things in the first place? Babel, and Egypt. . .that massacre, and now *this?* What does it all have to do with that walking nightmare in the cave? How does this reveal its supposed greatness?"

Gorgathuus stood silent, his amusement obvious.

"Why didn't Samson hear me?" Paradine asked his host. "Or that guard? They weren't deaf."

"*No one* hears you," Gorgathuus said. "No one sees you. Not here, not in Babel, not in Egypt. No one but *me*, anyway."

"Why don't they?"

"Are you *really* this dense? That is such a disappointment."

A tremendous rumble sounded from above, deafening and growing louder. Debris rained upon them as the walls shook, toppling stones from mortar that for centuries had held them. Shadows danced as the torch mountings loosened and fell.

"We are done here!" Gorgathuus shouted, grabbing Paradine by the arm as the ceiling collapsed. With a fading roar of stone upon stone, the prison broke into nothingness.

● ● ●

The cries of battle filled his ears.

Paradine dove to the ground, taking refuge behind a fallen tree trunk as all around him the war raged. For as far as he could see in the gray, rain-misted distance, soldiers clashed in hand-to-hand combat. One army was clad in silver helmets and blue tunics, over which were worn leather-strapped harnesses bearing armor plates. Their legs were covered by additional lengths of polished armor, which ran from the ankle to the knee.

The other combatants, clad in red, wore bronze helmets and

heavy armor of interlinked scales, which covered their upper bodies. Shin guards of bronze protected their legs. He recognized the second faction with little difficulty.

The Philistines.

"Get up from there," barked Gorgathuus, who wielded a huge bladed weapon akin to a battle axe. "Only I can harm you here."

Paradine rose from his place of seclusion in time to see his guide swing the great blade, savagely felling one enemy after another. Everywhere, swords clashed and shields shattered. Spears arced overhead, seldom missing their target.

Repulsed by the butchery around him, Paradine averted his eyes. Despite the apparent truth that he could not be injured, he kept low, creeping cautiously toward Gorgathuus, who was engaged in single combat. But it was the man who fought alongside the familiar warrior who drew the teacher's attention.

He was every bit as big as Gorgathuus, though apparently much younger. His face was boyish, his hair dark, his eyes wild. The two behemoths dwarfed every other man on the field, and only they wielded the huge, deadly axes, for no one else was large enough or strong enough to do so.

The carnage was absolute and horrible, but Paradine, shielded by his detachment, soon found himself unable to look away. It was all so real, yet so unreal. The two giants fighting side by side made for an incredible sight as they drove forward into the advancing lines. They swung their blades as if harvesting wheat, and their adversaries fell just as surely.

It became a rout. The warriors in blue could not stand up to the fierceness of the Philistine onslaught. Dismembered bodies covered the darkened ground so densely that Paradine found it difficult to walk without stepping on them.

A trumpet sounded in the distance. At once, the adversaries

retreated, running as quickly as their armor-laden legs would carry them. A cheer rose from the Philistines, who knew the day was theirs.

Paradine gingerly approached Gorgathuus, who, like his protégé, stood covered in enemy blood, his axe raised high in triumph. After watching the retreating forces for a moment, they turned and headed back in the direction of their camp, kicking the fallen soldiers in blue along the way.

"Where are we?" Paradine asked, struggling to keep up. "Who are those people?"

"The pass at Aphek," Gorgathuus replied, "and no one of any importance."

As he walked, Paradine looked down no more than he had to, for the grim carnage of war was strewn everywhere.

In silence, he followed the two giants out of the field of battle and into the Philistine camp. The wounded were looked after in a wide, open area to one side, but the quality of the medical care was primitive and only the most minor of injuries could successfully be treated. Groans of pain filled the air, along with shouted orders.

The camp rested on the shores of a narrow river, into which most of the soldiers dove in order to cleanse themselves. As they washed their armor, blades, shields, and bodies, the gently flowing waters were tinged red. Many of the men splashed like children at play, while others lay back on the riverbank and rested.

Gorgathuus was one of those who went into the water. Paradine stood on the shore, watching the man as he ducked under and reemerged, refreshed.

"Who was that other army?" Paradine repeated.

"The scourge of Philistia," he said. "The Israelites."

Paradine turned to look back over the hilly meadows where so many lay dead.

"There must be thousands of them dead," he said.

"Easily."

"Why are you fighting them? What did they do?"

"They live," Gorgathuus said. "That is reason enough."

The sun was beginning to set. The light rain had stopped, but still the clouds persisted, hiding the stars. Smoke rose from the mess tent, signaling the nearness of the evening meal. As darkness descended, a signal was given, and the troops gathered for their rations. Bread, cheese, and lamb were provided to the soldiers, and little would go to waste.

Gorgathuus reclined on the hillside, eating greedily and washing down each bite with a fermented beverage that Paradine did not recognize. Next to him was the other giant, also gorging himself.

Paradine sat nearby, watching the two.

"Who is that?" he asked Gorgathuus, indicating the other giant.

"A young soldier I am training in the ways of war," the man answered proudly, gulping from his flagon. "He was most inspiring today, was he not? He will make a fine warrior, and very soon."

"He's as big as you are," Paradine commented.

"Yes. . .the Philistines are fortunate to have two such fighters within their ranks. There are few of us left."

Paradine watched the young soldier as he quickly downed a great deal of food. A loud and resounding belch followed, then another.

"You must forgive the manners of Goliath," Gorgathuus laughed. "He has never been one to worry about appearances."

Paradine was amazed.

Goliath!

"*The* Goliath? of Gath?"

"Is there another?" laughed Gorgathuus.

Paradine rose and drew nearer the huge man. "He can't see me, right?"

"Again. . .only I can see you."

In astonishment, Paradine walked right up to the legendary man and studied his features, his clothing, everything about him.

"Amazing," he said. "Until now, I was certain he was nothing but a myth. To see him lounging there like that, as big as life. . . . No," he corrected himself, "*bigger* than life."

"All myth is founded in fact," Gorgathuus said. "But in the case of my protégé, no myth is involved."

Paradine walked around the camp, examining it in minute detail. No museum, no textbook, no scholar anywhere in the world knew as much about the Philistines as he did at that moment, as it played before him in seeming reality. Tents, tools, oil lamps, cooking utensils, provisions, weapons, armor, everything—he worked to memorize every feature.

Darkness fell, but less than two hours later, morning suddenly appeared again. Seeing Gorgathuus rising from his sleeping mat, Paradine knew he had jumped directly from the moment when the man had fallen asleep to the instant when he awoke the next morning.

His mind; his rules.

The sun broke over a clearing sky. A few high clouds gleamed golden in the east as the early light increased.

Very quickly, the army was dressed and ready for battle. Those who had not lived through the night were buried in hastily dug graves, while the surviving injured were loaded into wagons for transport back to Gaza.

A trumpet sounded in the distance.

"It is time," Gorgathuus said. "It begins again."

"They are fools if they think today will be any different," Goliath said, polishing the tip of the huge spear he held.

"Let them come. . .the sooner the world is rid of their kind, the better."

The soldiers formed ranks and advanced. Paradine marched alongside Gorgathuus and Goliath, fearing the bloodbath that surely would come.

"I want to sit this one out," he said, trying not to sound like a coward.

"You do not wish to witness the glory of battle?"

"I got enough of that yesterday."

Gorgathuus, clearly annoyed, nonetheless consented. "Very well. I had hoped you would prove to be a stronger man, but remain here if you must."

Paradine stopped in his tracks, stepped out of formation, and took a seat on a nearby outcropping of rock. The warriors continued on, their footfalls still heavy as they marched up and over the distant hills. No sooner had Gorgathuus disappeared from sight than the sun jumped to the other end of the sky, coming to rest at a point low above the western horizon.

A horn sounded. The army was returning.

Their numbers seemed barely to have decreased at all. Paradine saw the wounded being carried on captured wagons and horse-drawn sleds, but something else caught his eye as it glinted under the warm, orange rays of the sun.

He ran to the camp and stood near the mess tent. As the soldiers neared, great excitement arose among those who had remained behind. The men began to point and cheer and sing songs of glory.

Moments later, Paradine knew why.

The returning Philistines bore upon a flatbed wagon the

most sacred possession of the Israelites, the one object around which the worship of their God revolved.

"Praise be to Dagon!" they shouted. "He is mightier than the gods of the Israelites, and has delivered unto us the greatest of victories!"

Paradine approached as the wagon came to a stop. Weaving through the assembling crowd, he came face-to-face with the greatest archeological treasure known to modern man, a fabled object, long lost and feared destroyed. As Paradine's eyes beheld its magnificence, he could scarcely believe them. Covered in pure gold, it gleamed in the light, containing in silence the power of the ages.

The ark of the covenant!

"Dagon was with us," one soldier called out, "and they fell beneath our feet. We destroyed their forces and moved directly into their camp, and thirty thousand perished at our hands!"

Thirty thousand?

Paradine was astonished. "But, why was this treasure out there, so near the battlefield? Why wasn't it safely behind the lines?"

"Even there, it would not have been safe," Gorgathuus boasted, leading his guest away from the ark, away from the others.

Another soldier spoke up, shouting out to the crowd. "We heard them speak with great fear. After losing so many men yesterday, they trembled at the sight of us, expecting this day to bring utter defeat. So, their precious ark was brought from Shiloh, as if through it their ridiculous gods would empower them against us. But their gods trembled before ours, and we carried the day! We have captured the heart and soul of the Israelites, and soon their lands will be ours as well. . .and we will wipe them from the face of the earth."

Paradine stood with Gorgathuus, staring from a distance at the ark's ornate detail and exquisite beauty. He could have spent weeks just looking at it, he knew. He remembered the story of its sacred contents—one item in particular intrigued him. He entertained the thought of reaching out, lifting the cherubim-crowned lid, and taking a look inside.

Just imagine—the original stone tablets of Moses!

"I wouldn't," Gorgathuus laughed. "Not that you could."

"All right," Paradine insisted, clearly frustrated. "That's it. I want to know. . .*why not?* I can smell the food, but I can't eat it. I can't touch anything, yet I feel solid ground beneath my feet. What's going on? Why can no one but you see me or hear me?"

"Why should they?"

"Why can't they?" he repeated, more forcefully.

"Because," Gorgathuus said slowly, as if Paradine were dim, "they are but shadows."

Paradine scowled as the words rang with familiarity. The soldier looked at him expectantly, anticipating the realization he knew would come.

The scholar's mind raced as he recalled the words of another, words he had seen written, words he only recently had come to know: *These are but shadows of the things that have been—they have no consciousness of us!*

"Dickens," Paradine knew.

"Very good, Mr. Scrooge," Gorgathuus mocked. "And about time, I might add."

"That first night in the valley. . .I read that. . ."

Paradine looked at the huge man with realization and renewed horror.

"It's *you!*"

"A clever idea, was it not?" boasted the ancient being. "What better way to impress upon you my greatness, than by letting you experience it firsthand? You are living my glorious past, seeing and hearing and feeling my life through my memories of it."

"What happened?" a shocked Paradine asked. "How did you go from. . .from *this*. . ." He looked away, struggling to find words. "How did you become that cannibalistic abomination in the cave?"

"Abomination?" the soldier said with great amusement, leaning close. "Excuse me?"

"How did you become *Chayatocha?*"

"That will be all, I think," he replied, as if taking candy from a child. "For now."

The Philistine meadow slipped away. The cavern materialized around Paradine, and its cold, malodorous air once more filled his lungs.

The vile thing was settled on its throne before him.

Tired of playing games, Paradine glared into its yellow eyes.

"I ask again," Paradine pressed, "how did you become Chayatocha?"

The cave shook with obscene laughter.

"There is *no Chayatocha,"* it confessed. *"There never was."*

What?

"Then," Paradine asked, *"what are you?"*

The being considered him for a moment, as if trying to decide whether to spoil a surprise.

"When we came to this valley," it began, *"we moved silently and unseen through the forests. We watched the native people and adopted the legend they had created. We then filled a role, becoming the thing they most feared."*

"Why?"

"Because we enjoyed it," it smiled. *"Seeing them running around*

196

like that. It was like putting a stick in an anthill. Over a period of months, they lived their worst nightmare, as we used their greatest fears against them." Terrifying laughter filled the cavern. *"You are all such poor reflections of what you once were. . .puny things waiting to be led around by the nose."*

"So you said," Paradine recalled. "But the old man. . .he told me the life spirits protect him from you, and keep him fed, and heal him. He's been performing that drum ritual all his life. . . ."

Again the being laughed, loud and long. The echoing sound was terrifying.

"Meet the life spirits," it said, throwing its arms wide.

"You? Why?"

"What fun would it be, with no cage to rattle every now and then? He is a pet, nothing more." Paradine began to realize the full horror of the situation.

"When the old man tried to kill himself. . .tried to slit his wrists. . ."

"We could not have him running out on us, now could we?" The thing looked away, toward the Indian village. *"But now that we have you, we really do not need him anymore. . . ."*

"Please. . .don't!"

"Why should we let him continue his miserable existence? He lives in ignorance and superstition. He can never appreciate what we are. . . who we are. . ."

"Why do you stay here? Why not just leave. . .go where intelligent men abound?"

"We have our reasons."

"Why are you still alive after all this time? If you *aren't* a spirit. . .if you were once a man—"

"A god!" the being shouted.

"A god, then," the man echoed, "how is it you're still alive?"

It rushed forward, knocking him against a pile of bones with a swipe of its hand. It leaned over him, its eyes ablaze.

"That," it slowly said, *"we will* not *tell you."*

After a beat, it backed away, leaving Paradine to catch his breath.

"Who are you," the man asked, "that you should live so long?"

The being turned away, took a few thunderous steps, then whirled to face him and began to speak with great pride in its voice.

"Legends have been written of us and retold through the centuries." It looked away once more, its eyes embracing the sight of its gathered treasures.

"We are Gilgamesh, and Garaatoth, and Quetzalcoatl, and Bran. . . a hundred other names. We have fought in a thousand wars, ruled scores of kingdoms, and have walked all the lands of the earth. We fill the histories of this planet. . .we have shaped the course of mankind again and again! We are he who cannot die; he who will outlast the monuments we built in Egypt, and Machu Picchu, and Chichen Itza, and Teotihuacan! We are he who will devour the world."

"And yet—" Paradine began.

It spun upon him. *"What?"*

"You now confine yourself to a small, dark valley in the middle of nowhere, and have for the better part of a century."

The being gave no reply, but in silence retook its place on its throne.

"So, why *are* you here?" Paradine asked.

It picked up and fingered a rib bone. *"We command the winds, and the seas, and the earth. We go wherever we please."*

"And yet—"

The creature flew into a rage.

"*Go!*" it commanded. "*Pray you live until tomorrow. Pray you will hear our voice again, and that we will choose to honor you further.*"

Knowing he may have pushed too far, Paradine grabbed his lantern and quickly exited the cavern. The more distance he put between himself and the beast, the better he felt.

Why doesn't it leave? What's holding it here?

Descending the mountainside, he strained to spot Seukani's house in the distance, hoping perhaps a light might be burning there. There was none.

I've got to warn him...

As quickly as his weary legs would carry him, he headed toward the village.

Chapter 12

Paradine awoke from a sound sleep.
For a moment, he glanced around in panic, not knowing where he was. His heart pounded

Then he remembered.

He lay stretched out on a sleeping mat, which he had found stored in the home of Seukani. The old man had not been there when he arrived.

He sat up and rubbed his hair, wishing for a bath, or a minute under a waterfall, or a good rain—anything to wash away the grime of the ages.

Did all of that really happen? Did I really see those things?

He checked his watch.

Seven thirty-two.

The sky outside was as dark as ever, but the timepiece's sun/moon indicator told him it was morning. He rose and stretched, scanning the room for something to eat. A couple of logs added to the fire soon brought it to full vigor, warming and lighting the room more to his satisfaction.

As he dug through Seukani's battered pots and pans, his eyes fell upon a pocket watch nestled amid a few small personal items piled to one side. It had tarnished badly but seemed in fair enough condition.

He picked it up, opened it, and found it had stopped running. An attempt at winding it was fruitless.

How long have you had this? he wondered. *Looks like it was a nice one.*

Replacing it, he returned his attention to the matter of food. One cloth pouch hanging from a wooden peg held several pieces of dried meat; another contained what looked like hardtack.

Close enough.

A wooden crock with a lid held water. Scooping some into a metal cup, Paradine took the food and crossed to a low table nearby. Folding his legs beneath him, he found a position that was comfortable, at least for a little while.

"Where are you, my friend?" he wondered aloud concerning the Indian, even as a thought occurred to him.

Lucky, was it you? Did you take him somewhere? Back to that upside-down wagon, maybe?

"I'm not sure he wouldn't have been safer right here. . . ."

He ate some meat and bread, washing it down fairly often, of necessity. As he ate, he studied the room—the hangings and carvings, the structure itself.

It looks sturdy, I'll give him that. . .

The air in the room began to move. Paradine looked up to

see if the door had been opened, but found it closed as tightly as ever.

That's strange. . .

Again the air stirred, as if someone were walking past. An area of cold enveloped him—by extending his arms, he could sense its limits.

"Mr. Paradine," a voice sounded.

The scholar jumped, realizing that it had not been an audible voice but a thought echoing within his skull.

"Who are you?"

"We are they who conquer death," came the words, in a whisper—yet not a solitary whisper, but a unity of voices. Beautiful, melodic, like music.

"I don't understand."

"You will. We will speak with you again when the time is right, and that time is soon. Do not fear."

The cold air warmed. All was still.

"Hello?" Paradine tried.

Silence.

He went back to his meal, hoping he still was sane.

◎ ◎ ◎

Rifle in hand, Lucky moved with precision through the darkness, his way sure, his jaw set. He knew that the powerful evil that had claimed the valley would take other lives if not stopped.

He crossed through the makeshift graveyard, careful to avoid the open pits that were everywhere. With great sadness he looked upon the ravaged markers, knowing each name, knowing the fate they had shared.

Time was short. He left the dead behind and continued on.

◉ ◉ ◉

Come to us.

Paradine stood before the throne.

"At least now I know what to call you," he said.

"Once more you will journey back with us," said the inhuman creature.

"What I don't know is what happened to you. How does a man become. . .like. . .like. . .*you?*"

"We ascended to godhood," it said. *"We are eternal."*

"I never knew the gods were so hideous," Paradine said, more angry than frightened.

Gorgathuus exploded from the bone pile, pinning Paradine in an instant. Its breath froze the sweat on his forehead as it leaned close, its eyes ablaze, its hand against his chest.

"You will witness all that we now will show you," it bellowed, *"and then, you will die."* It smiled cruelly, its lips parting to reveal jagged teeth and black gums. *"But first, your wife and son will be torn limb from limb and devoured as you watch. All who remain in this place will perish in agony and terror. . .and* you *brought it upon them."*

The blue light rose. Paradine felt himself falling.

When his feet found solid ground, a broad expanse of stars shone above. The air was hot and still and sticky.

He stood outside the gate of an ancient city, surrounded by thousands of soldiers carrying weapons and torches. Covered in bronze plate armor, they bore gleaming broadswords and round wooden shields, their heads hidden by intricate helmets of metal and leather. It was not an army he had seen before, nor one he recognized from his books of antiquity.

High earthen ramps had been erected against the wall and thousands had already breached the city's defenses. Still more soldiers surged up the ramps, meeting little resistance. For the moment, the massive gates were still sealed.

And then, as Paradine watched raptly, they began to part. Slowly at first, with a thunderous groan, the invaders opened the gate from the inside. A cheer went up from the throng, who raised their swords into the air in triumph and charged forward.

"Victory," said a voice he knew too well.

He turned to find Gorgathuus approaching from behind him. The warrior was clad in the same armor as the others, but with a few decorative differences that revealed his great rank. Most striking were the physical changes he had undergone since Paradine had last seen him.

His eyes, jaundiced and wet, rested in dark sockets. His skin was leathery and rough. Each breath sounded loudly.

Seeking to attack the future monster, Paradine tried to pick up a heavy branch that lay beside the road. His hands found no substance—he could not lift it.

"You cannot harm me here," the giant said. "You are nothing."

The teacher backed away, his anger building.

"If you harm my wife or son," he threatened, "I *will* find a way to destroy you. If it takes the rest of my life. . ."

"You would need more time than that," said Gorgathuus, with great confidence. "Much more."

They stood facing each other for a moment. Paradine studied the soldier's features more closely.

"You don't look so good," he said, taking satisfaction in the observation. "On the other hand, you're going to look a *lot* worse."

The warrior ignored the comment.

"So, what do I call you now?" Paradine asked, with heavy sarcasm. "Caesar? Zeus? Alexander the Great?"

"These people know me as Samgarnebo," he boasted, "a

general in the army of the great King Nebuchadnezzar. These are my men. . ." He indicated the troops around him. "The Chaldeans, the mightiest fighting force in all the land."

Gorgathuus spun Paradine and shoved him forward, and together they passed through the gate.

"Welcome to Jerusalem, Mr. Paradine," he said, his eyes aglow with triumph. "For thirty months we have surrounded her, cut her off, starved her people. And now, this night, she falls to us. In mere days, she will be no more."

"Then, this is 586 B.C.," Paradine recalled.

"July 18," Gorgathuus nodded, "as you mark time."

They moved through the streets, flowing among the soldiers, who knocked down doors and set ablaze every home they came upon. Battering rams tore down walls that had stood for ages. Many who had survived the prolonged onslaught fled in a vain attempt to escape the city, only to be captured and dragged into holding areas. Noblemen, many of whom attempted to buy their way out of capture, were put to death on the spot. Those skilled in working with wood, clay, or metal were taken into exile, their talents to be put to use for Babylon. Many surrendered as the Chaldeans had instructed, knowing their lives would be spared if they swore allegiance to Nebuchadnezzar.

Screams echoed in Paradine's ears. The crisp roar and golden light of uncontrolled fire raged all around him.

"They should have listened," Gorgathuus said. "They were warned. Their own prophets told them their beloved city would fall if they did not yield to us." He inhaled deeply, savoring the air. "The evil of this place is delicious. . .the air still hangs heavy with the scent of the children they sacrificed to the false gods they created, the stones and the trees and the stars. The God of their fathers has forsaken them. . .and soon, they will be no more."

"That isn't true," Paradine said, choking amid the smoke.

"Isn't it?" the man laughed. "Their time is short. . .they will rebuild this place, only to lose it again, once and for all. . ."

A soldier ran up to Gorgathuus and bowed in salute.

"Sir," he said, trying to catch his breath, "King Zedekiah has been captured."

"Within the palace?"

"No, sir. He was caught attempting to cross the plain at Jericho. It is believed he escaped the city by way of the king's garden. . .the gate there was unguarded."

"Who is the fool who failed to secure that gate?"

"I do not know, sir," the soldier answered fearfully.

"Has Nebuzaradan been informed?"

"Yes, sir. . .the captain has ordered that Zedekiah and his sons be taken at once to Riblah, where our great king awaits."

"Very good," Gorgathuus smiled. "You may go."

"Yes, sir," the man said, bowing as he departed. "Thank you, sir."

Gorgathuus took up a torch and laughed as he began to set fire to anything that would burn—wood, hay, window curtains, even fallen bodies ignited at the touch of his torch. The firelight reflecting in his wide eyes illuminated the depths of his wickedness, a malevolence that Paradine knew only increased with time. The teacher could only stand and watch as the city around him burned, and the thunder of the battering rams sounded again and again from different sections of Jerusalem.

Hearing a human sound, Paradine moved ahead of the Chaldean general. In a doorway huddled a woman, cradling her child in fear. She began to beg for her life.

Her pleas were answered by Gorgathuus's sword.

Paradine cursed his host, who only laughed more loudly.

He turned away and leaned into a wall, hating the scene playing out before him. As he paced his breathing, trying to calm himself, he felt a presence waft over him.

"Mr. Paradine," sounded the soft, melodious voices again.

"Yes?" he whispered. "I hear you."

"We have chosen you, Mr. Paradine."

"I don't want to be chosen," he replied. "For *anything*. That thing in the cave chose me, and now—"

"The thing in the cave is not a concern."

Paradine paused, his interest piqued.

"Go on."

"Gorgathuus is trapped within the valley of darkness. Physically, he is free to leave, but he chooses not to, for he can no longer walk among men as one of them. Because of what he has become, he is a pariah, isolated and alone."

Paradine glanced over at the general, who was busy smashing pottery with his sword.

"What happened to him?"

"It is we who have sustained him," the plural whisper continued, *"allowing him to be a part of some of the greatest civilizations the world has known. But as a result of that immortality, he became the disfigured monster you know, the malignant beast that holds the valley captive."*

"You did this to him?"

"His physical transformation came as a result of his own corrupted flesh. Our energies merely amplified it. He has used our power to do great harm. . .it is the means by which he ensnares his victims and keeps them shrouded in darkness. Without us, he is nothing."

"So what do you want from me?"

"Just as he is trapped within the valley, so we are trapped within him. We do not wish to live out the centuries in a secluded cavern,

away from the things of man. Nor do we wish to endure any longer our existence inside this grotesque creature.

"We desire a man of intellect, a man of promise. We seek a new host, one willing to venture forth into the great cities of the world. . . New York, Paris, London. . .where so many opportunities await."

"Opportunities for what?"

"For interaction with your fellow men. We wish to walk among the scholars of your world, to teach and to learn, to experience once more the beauty your world has to offer."

Paradine drew a deep breath.

"Who *are* you, exactly?"

"We are they who have traveled this earth since its creation, spirit beings who desire a host in order to live among men, as one of them."

"Desire, or require?"

"Does it matter?"

Paradine, thinking hard, absently rubbed the wall with his fingertips.

"I don't know. . ."

"We offer you much, Daniel."

"You're still within him? Even now?"

"Yes."

"He doesn't know you're speaking with me," Paradine said. "Does he?"

"He does not."

"So, you want to leave him. . .and you want me to be your new host."

"Think of all you could accomplish, all you could learn, with untold millennia open before you. During this great age of enlightenment, you would come to know more than any man ever born."

"I appreciate the offer," Paradine said, "but I'm really thinking *no.*"

"With our help, you will cure all disease. . .end all suffering. . . solve every problem of the world. . ."

He began to weaken. They sensed it.

"Everything the world can offer will be yours for the asking. Wealth, power, influence. . .women, should you desire them. . ."

His mind flashed to the voluptuous harlots of Babel.

"Paradine!" shouted Gorgathuus, slapping the man's shoulder with the back of a hand. "What's wrong with you?"

"Nothing," the startled teacher answered, jolted from his reverie.

"Come," the general ordered. "We must return to the northern gate."

The giant led Paradine through the ruins, checking open doors and windows for anyone who might still be hiding.

"Looks like they've all gone," he commented, "one way or another."

Paradine barely heard his words. He was deep in thought, trying to make sense of what he had heard.

Me? They want me?

As they passed the royal palace, its blackened facade consumed in flame, one of its outer walls collapsed into a shattered heap. Paradine, feeling the intense heat of the fire on his face and hands, hurried past and moved into the shadow of a potter's shed which had not yet been destroyed.

"I wouldn't stand there," Gorgathuus said, setting alight its wooden frame.

It was a walk through hell. The heat was unbearable. The sky glowed orange and angry, the smoke blanketing the entirety of the city.

Paradine, his mind fully occupied, stumbled more than once along the way.

No wonder he refers to himself as "we". . .who knows how many of those things live within him?

Finally they reached the Middle Gate and exited the city. On the surrounding hillsides, Paradine saw thousands of Jewish prisoners being led away in chains, most of whom were doomed to walk the two hundred miles to Babylon, where they would assume new lives as servants of their captors.

"Fully a third died of disease or starvation before we ever entered the city," Gorgathuus said, pleased with the battle tactics he had helped to devise. "Another third died trying to fight us— as if they stood a chance. The remainder are those we are taking into exile, and the few we leave behind to live like animals amid the rubble."

"You must be proud," Paradine said, struggling to contain his anger.

"War is war," said the Chaldean mercenary, "and it is glorious."

Paradine began to say something in reply, but the words were carried away on waves of silence as the dizziness enveloped him again. He closed his eyes.

When he opened them, seconds later, he still stood at the gates of Jerusalem. But it was a vastly different city that rose before him, shining and white and spectacular, risen from the ashes of the Babylonian conquest.

"Wow," he said, breathlessly.

He stepped forward, through the soaring, open doors and into the entry plaza. It still was night—torches and lamps burned brightly, lighting his way. Except for the song of a few night birds, all was quiet. The tranquility was a welcome change from the carnage he had just witnessed.

Most of the people were asleep, their window shutters open to admit the cool, refreshing air. He glanced up into the night sky

211

and immediately recognized the constellations of late autumn. Leo, Gemini, Taurus, and Orion greeted him like old friends, and he welcomed the sight. It was wonderful, the first real moment of peace he had experienced since his ordeal began. All was calm.

Too calm.

Wait a minute—

"I know you're here," he said, not too loudly. "You *have* to be."

A figure emerged from the shadows.

"Indeed," said Gorgathuus, his voice deeper and more inhuman than ever. The huge man was shrouded in dark, heavy robes. A wide hood concealed his face. Only his hands were visible, protruding from beneath the roughly woven fabric, and they betrayed the fact of his further degeneration.

"Come," he said, "we have a short journey yet to make."

"How far are we going?"

"Only a few miles."

The road was deserted. Behind them, Jerusalem soon vanished from sight. At times, Paradine had trouble keeping up with his host.

"You walk too fast," he complained.

"My stride is longer," Gorgathuus said. "The fault is yours."

"Fault? What fault?"

"Your size."

"That again?" Paradine groaned. "So we used to be bigger. So what happened?"

"You angered God. . .refused to be His pawns. He punished you with diminished size and a shortened lifespan."

"Did he really—?"

"Daniel," the spoken music interrupted. He looked away.

"Yes," he whispered, wary of Gorgathuus overhearing.

"*You need not speak aloud.*"

"Even so," thought Paradine, "Gorgathuus might overhear and—"

"*He cannot now hear your thoughts, or ours. We have shielded your mind from him.*"

"What do you want?"

"*Have you considered our offer?*"

"I told you. . .the answer's *no.*"

"*Do not decide rashly,*" the plurality warned. "*There is much at stake.*"

"For you, maybe. . ."

"*For many. Think of the millions who will die of diseases you could have cured, or in conflicts your wisdom could have prevented.*"

"Look, why don't you just go find someone else."

"*We have chosen you.*"

"What if I don't change my mind? Will you just take me anyway?"

"*No.*"

"Why not?"

"*We need a receptive host. Were we to enter the unwilling, a continual battle would ensue. The conflict of wills would be devastating. . . the result would be a man driven insane. An animal. We do not wish a drooling beast, whose mind and hands would be useless to us.*"

"You're talking about *possession,*" Paradine said, as the realization dawned.

"*In a manner of speaking.*"

"I let you in, and you take over."

"*No. . .we work together as one. We could not overpower your will, just as we cannot overpower that of Gorgathuus. This is why we could never stop him from continuing the cruelty he has unleashed upon the world.*"

"Can't you just leave him? Stop him that way?"

"We must have a vessel."

"Why did you enter a soldier in the first place?"

"It was a different time, then. The world was a vastly different place. Power was the key to all things in those days, just as intellect is today."

"So," he understood, "the biblical stories about demonic possession are true. Demons *do* exist. . .don't you?"

"Daniel," the voices implored, *"you can see to it that Gorgathuus never kills another living soul. No longer will anyone die at his hands. . .including your wife and child."*

"I thought demons were evil," Paradine said.

"We are engaged in a conflict. You have listened to the half-truths of the other side. We are spirit beings who desire only to move among men, and help them, and learn from them."

"You're telling me that God is a liar."

"We are telling you that he does not care for his creation as he would have you believe. His ego outweighs his compassion. Look at what he unleashed upon the world of Noah's day. Later, as you saw, he looked the other way as the Chaldeans destroyed the city of his people. Since the beginning, he has allowed suffering to fill the world, all for his own selfish pleasure. We stood against him. . .we wanted only to help mankind, and not see them have to endure pain and loss. For this, we were banished from the dwelling place of the spirits."

Paradine, hard pressed to argue, struggled to get his mind around it all. Only days before, he had not even believed in the existence of God or demons. The spirit realm, he had been certain, was a fabrication rooted in superstition and opposed to science.

Now, he was conversing with that realm.

"How do I know you won't turn me into a thing like Gorgathuus became?"

"He is descended from a race of giants who destroyed their seed through continual inbreeding. Too late, we discovered that his flesh was not stable enough to contain our energies for such a prolonged period. Your kind has not suffered such corruption. You will appear the same five thousand years from now as you do today. Still young, still vital, still alive."

Immortality!

Paradine thought hard. He knew the offer they made carried risk, but the benefits were extraordinary.

"You're telling me for certain that my wife and son are safe?"

"We are."

"And if I agree to this, you will deliver them safely to me? We'll all be able to leave the valley and go on with our lives, and Gorgathuus will never touch us?"

"You have our pledge, Mr. Paradine. You will depart in security and begin an adventure of which you would never have dared to dream."

"What about the others trapped in there. . .those who still are alive?"

"They will go with you, of course. Their lives also will be preserved."

Never in his life had he made a snap decision. He would not start now.

"I'm sorry. . .I still need to think this over."

"We understand," the voices gently said. *"Such a commitment is not to be entered into lightly. We await your decision."*

The voices faded and were gone. Paradine glanced at the nocturnal terrain around him, with no memory of having walked there.

"You are quiet," Gorgathuus commented.

"Lot on my mind, I guess," the teacher nervously said. "Where does this road lead?"

"One can follow it all the way to Gaza, passing through Hebron along the way."

A village appeared ahead, bathed in the light of the stars and moon. It was a place of moderate size, with scores of dwelling places lining the road. Stone watchtowers stood overlooking the surrounding meadows. In the distance, a conical hill rose, topped by a citadel.

"What's that up there?" asked Paradine.

"The winter palace of the king. Most spectacular."

"You've been there?"

"Oh, yes."

They entered the village proper. Gorgathuus led them down an intersecting street and into what clearly was a residential area. There, as in Jerusalem, all were sleeping.

"Now what?" Paradine asked.

"We wait."

"What is this place? Why are we here?"

"Patience."

They stood in silence. Paradine craned his neck and studied the stars once again, comforted by their brilliance.

And then, he heard them.

The pounding beat of horses' hooves sounded in the distance, growing ever closer, ever louder. Paradine looked up at Gorgathuus—beneath his hood he was smiling.

Soldiers flooded the streets, a few dismounting and drawing swords. As Paradine watched, the soldiers burst into one home after another, only to emerge moments later, their swords bloodied. Screams arose from all directions, echoing in the night.

As one soldier broke down the door of a house near him, Paradine rushed forward and peered through the window. Before his eyes, the already bloodied man pulled a baby from the arms of a panicked mother, ran him through with his blade, and dropped the sundered body to the floor. The woman screamed in horror, diving upon the tiny form of her child, sobbing in agony.

"No!" Paradine cried out. He ran to one house, then the next, trying to bang on their doors in warning. But the phantom wood made no sound beneath his fists.

"Run!" he shouted, straining his throat with the effort. "Hide your children! They're killing the children!"

No one heard him.

They are but shadows—

His eyes filled with tears of anger and frustration.

"Stop! Don't do this!" he screamed in futility, turning from one soldier to the next, but they just ran past and sometimes even through him in the execution of their terrible orders.

Paradine turned, ran up to Gorgathuus, and grabbed him by the front of his cloak.

"You have to stop this!" he begged. "You they can see and hear! Stop them!"

"Why would I want to do that?" laughed the fiend. "It was *my* idea."

"*What?*"

"A well-placed whisper in the mind of a man can accomplish much," gloated the monster, "and Herod was most receptive. It would seem a prophesied 'messiah' was born in this little town but recently, and the good king was worried about losing his crown."

Paradine whirled, seeing the place anew with knowing eyes.

Bethlehem!

He scanned the sky. No unique, brilliant star shone above. It had come and gone, long before.

"History repeats itself!" Gorgathuus gloried. "Is it not a

beautiful thing? As happened in Egypt, now happens again." He closed his eyes, as if savoring a memory. "These Hebrews are much too prolific for their own good."

Paradine recalled the story of the Exodus, the command from Pharaoh that all male infants be drowned at birth. Until that moment, it had been nothing but cold, sterile history. Now, it writhed with anguished death throes and a mother's bitter tears.

"You took part in *that?*"

"A revolt was in the offing, and Amenhotep knew it. What better preventive measure than to reduce their numbers and yet preserve your workforce by taking those who yet offered nothing? Thousands were cast into the Nile as we enforced the edict, but we were not thorough enough—had Moses also died then, much would have been different." He listened to the screams as they filled the town. "Such music, just as before. In a single night, hundreds perish. . .and a whisper is as lethal as a thousand swords."

The ancient being laughed, long and loud and hard.

Paradine turned away, dropped to his knees, and wept.

The dusty ground beneath him, the city around him, the night sky above him all blurred and faded into nothingness.

Chapter 13

When Paradine lifted his head, he found himself in a lush, green meadow. The sun, still low in the morning sky, cast long shadows. He turned, wiped the wetness from his face, and realized the city wall of Jerusalem stood some distance behind him. The grasses moved in gentle waves, and emerald trees filled with new blossoms fluttered in the cool breeze. Their branches were laden with young fruit and singing birds—and one very dead man.

Paradine rose to his feet and rushed forward, toward the gnarled tree that rose at the edge of the verdant plateau. From a low, straining branch hung a length of braided rope, the lower end of which was wrapped around the neck of a dark-haired man whose face was a portrait of grief. His lips were dark, his tongue swollen. His unseeing eyes stared at the sprawling city. He swung slightly, catching the wind as it rolled up the hillside. The dry, narrow bough from which he hung, stressed to its limits, creaked with each movement.

Paradine, forgetting himself, reached up that he might grab the man around the legs and relieve the stress on the rope, but his phantom arms merely passed through the body. He backed away.

Why did you do this? What could have been so bad that—

"What, indeed." The voice had a peculiar, inherent echo.

Paradine turned to see Gorgathuus standing in the shadows of a nearby olive tree. He repeatedly tossed something small a few inches into the air and caught it again. Each time, a sharp, familiar noise rang out.

"What did you do?" Paradine asked fearfully.

"Whispers," Gorgathuus smiled. "They can accomplish so much."

Paradine returned his gaze to the dead man, just in time to see the branch splinter and give way. The body fell, toppling over the edge of the plateau. Paradine rushed forward and saw the corpse strike one boulder, then another before coming to rest in an awkward tangle a couple of dozen feet downhill. Its abdomen had ruptured upon impact with the jagged rocks, spilling its contents onto the thriving spring meadow.

Gorgathuus walked over to the edge and glanced down.

"So sad," he said with false pity. "He showed such promise."

Paradine looked upon his host with disgust. He noted the object in his hand—a small pouch of heavy blue fabric, laced closed at the top. It made a metallic sound.

"You'd think that such a devoted deed would have warranted much more than mere silver. . .and only thirty pieces, at that.

I mean, really. . .had I known that was all they would pay, I might not have bothered."

"Judas," Paradine said, recalling the story he had read in the Bible. "He hanged himself. . .fell headlong. . .and burst open."

"So it would seem."

Paradine noticed that the colossus physically had degenerated further since the last time he had seen him. His hands and face were covered in mottled gray flesh, with raised welts and what appeared to be open lesions. He carried a scent of sulfur. Paradine could only imagine the extent of the deformity concealed by the dark, heavy robes.

He eyed the blue pouch. "How did you get it? The silver?"

The corner of Gorgathuus's festering mouth turned up in a slight smile. "I made it mine on the way here. No sooner had the priests given it over to the potter's guild than I, shall we say, 'acquired' it. It will make a nice memento of my brief time with that *poor* soul."

The monster laughed, enjoying his own wordplay.

Paradine walked away from the edge of the hill. "How could you lead a dedicated follower into betrayal?"

"By knowing that the one thing he wanted more than anything was to see his country freed from Roman rule. He had become *so* disappointed in his 'messiah'. . .at every turn, the man to whom poor Judas had devoted so much time and effort refused to assume his rightful place. The fires of impatience flared. So, I put it into his mind that one way to force the issue would be to put his beloved teacher into a position where he would *have* to tell the Jews and Romans exactly who he was. Once he began to defend himself, given he truly *was* the messiah, it would be but a short step for him to assume his place on the throne, would it not? And if he was a *false* prophet, he would die. . .with no harm done."

Paradine was horrified.

"The ironic thing is, he never really believed in the man. *What fools these mortals be. . .*"

Paradine looked at the dead tree with its now broken limb. Something there spoke to him, in words he could not yet decipher. He turned away, trying to erase the image of the dead man, trying to force his mind into a more academic line of thought.

"Then, this is somewhere around A.D. 33. . ."

"Close," the beast corrected him. "Closer to 4000, actually. They don't set the clocks back for a while yet."

"And you brought me here because of what's about to happen."

"Tomorrow," grinned Gorgathuus. "Yes."

"Why? Why show me this?"

"These Hebrews have been a plague upon the world," Gorgathuus began, hatred in his voice. "They crippled and destroyed some of the greatest civilizations. . .the greatest men. . . ever to rise from the earth. Egypt, Philistia, all of Canaan." He grew angry. "Their King David and his men hunted down and slew my brethren: Sippai, and Lahmi, and all the sons of Ammon, the sons of Anak. And Goliath, who was as a son to me. . ."

Paradine saw the giant's eyes burn yellow.

"Tomorrow begins their final downfall," Gorgathuus said, the rage evident in his raspy voice, "and you shall be there to witness it, as was I!"

"Final?"

"Before this century is out, they will be scattered to the winds, never to rise again. What we did to their beloved city five hundred years ago will pale by comparison. Never again will a conqueror soften and allow their return to this land. . .never again will their temple stand upon this mountain, nor will their feet find safety here. I will see to that *personally.*"

Paradine looked toward the city. Its gates were open, its people moving to and fro with no understanding of the fateful day that would come upon them with the next sunrise.

And then, suddenly, that day had dawned.

Paradine, startled by the sudden shift in locale, fell back into the shaded entry of a residence, against its sealed door. He stood at the back of a crowd that lined a narrow, crowded street. All were abuzz with anticipation, craning their necks to look along the way, to catch a glimpse of—*something*.

Next to him, just a few feet away and beneath the overhang of a market, he spied Gorgathuus. Little of him was visible beneath his robes—even his hands were concealed. He stood well above those around him, as usual, and as a result drew unwanted attention. One man, possibly the shopkeeper, grew curious about the huge stranger standing behind the display of breads and grains and bent low for a better look up beneath his hood.

Paradine saw the man's eyes go wide.

"A leper. . . !"

The words were his last. Gorgathuus snapped his head to the side and glared at the man. Instantly, he fell back, clutching his throat, unable to utter another sound. Panicked, the baker turned, fell back through the open door of his shop, and vanished from sight.

Gorgathuus, more careful now to conceal himself, withdrew and chose a more secluded spot farther along the way.

And then, the crowd began to roar.

Paradine, taller than most of those who stood in front of him, managed a decent view despite his distance. Several soldiers came down the street, shoving the crowd back as they went, as if clearing the way. Their dress and armor, he knew, was Roman. They soon passed, revealing behind them the one for whom they ran interference.

When Paradine beheld the figure, his breath failed him.

The man came staggering down the center of the street, heavily burdened and visibly injured. The throng began to hurl things at him. Mock him. Strike him.

No. . .it can't be!

The bloodied figure drew near. His face, now barely human in appearance, was beaten, cut, and swollen. His lips were badly lacerated, with a few frontal teeth absent. He had the remnants of a beard, which hung in uneven tufts upon his jaw—much of it clearly had been pulled out by the roots. Upon his head had been tied a wide knot of stiff, thorny vines, which dug into his scalp, sending rivulets of blood coursing down his battered face and onto his neck and chest. His shoulders, arms, and legs bore the cruel signature of the Roman flagrum, a multi-tongued whip that tore into the flesh with barbs of metal and bone. His shoulders had been flayed open in places. His body was spattered with both the bright, glistening red of fresh flows and the darker grit of older wounds.

Each step was heavy and unsure. He bore upon his back a massive wooden beam more than six feet long, secured to his out-stretched arms with lengths of coarse rope. He labored to endure its weight, his legs quivering as if they might fail at any moment, sending him to the pavement. He gasped for air, his face a distorted grimace of agony.

Paradine, his eyes wet, looked away. Something deep within him sensed a conviction, as if his entire life were on trial. In a few moments, the man had passed by. The teacher then heard the thud of heavy wood being dropped onto paving stones, and the shouts of soldiers. The jeers of the crowd grew louder. After a brief interval, the gathered horde began to move along, following, leaving Paradine standing alone. He looked up, his vision blurred by tears, and saw Gorgathuus beckoning to him from the darkness of an alley.

"Come," he said, "you now will witness my most glorious victory!"

"I'm not going," Paradine said. "I don't care about God or the Jews, or what they have or haven't done. I'm tired of all this. I've seen enough killing to last me the rest of my life. I'm not going anywhere else with you."

"Yes," Gorgathuus said, his tone a threat, "you are."

"I told you. . .I've seen enough."

The monstrosity stepped closer and stood menacingly over Paradine.

"So," he growled, "you are ready to die then, here and now?"

Paradine swallowed hard, his eyes fixed on those of the reaper before him. After a long and terrifying moment, he looked away, cursed under his breath, and surrendered.

"Just get it over with."

They kept to the shadows, creeping along the outskirts as Gorgathuus did his best to avoid further contact with the populace. They soon came to a gate and slipped outside the city walls, where the going was more secretive.

"Stay with me," the beast warned. Paradine gave no reply, but followed close behind.

Making their way north, they came upon a rocky hill which overlooked the northern road leading from the city. Citizens had congregated in uneven groups at its base, on the unpaved thoroughfare below. A wide, well-traveled path curved up its western slope. Its summit was the highest point in Jerusalem.

And upon that summit, long before, a father of great faith

had been willing to offer his own son as a sacrifice.

Paradine's eyes fixed on the southern side of the hill, a wide expanse of white limestone originally exposed when blocks had been quarried for the building of Solomon's Temple.

Look at that. . .

Into the nearly vertical face, inadvertent chisels and the elements had carved a visage that was rough yet striking, that of a death's head. Eye sockets, nose, and clenched teeth all were there, startling and unforgettable.

No wonder they called it Golgotha. . .the "place of the skull."

He lifted his eyes to the plateau atop the hill. There, a framework of wooden posts rose, intended for a purpose he understood all too well. Roman soldiers milled about, busily carrying out their orders, their duty.

"We must hurry," Gorgathuus said. "We do not want to miss this."

They moved among the trees and came upon the downslope side of the hill, opposite the city. It, too, was covered with forest and vegetation, providing cover. Gorgathuus led Paradine upward, along its flanks.

Voices sounded in Paradine's mind.

"Daniel. . ."

"Yes?" he thought, again embracing the beauty of the spoken music.

"We must have an answer. Your time is short. In mere minutes, this journey of illusion will end, and you will find yourself back in the cavern. Once there, Gorgathuus will kill you, your wife, your son, and all who yet inhabit the valley. Only you can stop him. You must choose."

He listened.

"Allow us to come into you, and we will keep you and your family safe. No power on earth will touch you. Together, we will go forth

into the world and do great things."

"I still need time. . . ."

"Time is a luxury you do not have. Your life is in danger. . .and do not let an unfounded fear steal away the lives of your family."

The voices went silent, awaiting his decision.

The sound of hammers driving into iron echoed from the summit, punctuated by screams of pain.

"Ah," Gorgathuus said, "it begins."

Paradine and the cloaked colossus approached the top of the hill, coming around the unoccupied northern side. The pair remained in the shadow of the trees as the upper plateau came into view.

"Go on," the giant encouraged Paradine. "Get closer. Get a good view. You must witness the moment of their greatest defeat and my greatest victory."

"But, if *you* can't see it, *I* can't see it."

"I have access to eyes not my own. Go."

Even as the teacher climbed the final ten feet, three figures were lifted up into view and into place upon reinforced, upright posts. At first, he saw them only from behind. The battered man was in the center, facing the city, with the others to either side of him.

It was nine in the morning as Paradine crested the plateau. Cool breezes swept the hilltop, chilling him. He circled around in front of the victims, looking upon them with great sadness. Jeers rose from the road below—he turned to see those who had gathered there ridiculing the men and shouting obscenities.

Paradine's eyes found the place in each man's wrist where heavy iron nails had been driven through. Blood coursed down, dripping onto the ground. Their feet also, one atop the other, had been secured by spikes to the blocks of wood attached to the upright posts. Paradine was reminded of the totems he had seen on the dark lakeshore.

Soldiers hung wooden placards above each, stating in Hebrew, Greek, and Latin the crimes for which each man had been convicted. Even without Gorgathuus's knowledge base, Paradine could have read them, for he possessed a working knowledge of Latin. The two men on the outer crosses were thieves, but the placard over the head of the man in the middle bore witness to quite a different crime: JESUS THE NAZARENE, THE KING OF THE JEWS.

Several people milled about the foot of the crosses, most of whom were relatives of the crucified men. A centurion, standing guard against an untoward attack upon the convicted trio, kept everyone a spear's length away. The family members wept, striving through their tears to comfort their loved ones in their final moments.

The two thieves, even through their suffering, began to argue. The central figure turned His head toward one, spoke to him in words Paradine could not hear, then lowered His head and closed His eyes, as if conserving His remaining strength.

"Father," he said in a near whisper, "forgive them...they don't realize what they're doing."

He wore only a loincloth. His bloodstained outer garments had been taken from Him.

Paradine overheard a deep and prominent voice. He spotted a pair of Jewish leaders standing a short distance away, whose conversation carried across the hilltop.

"They say he saved others," one of them sneered. "If he's the Messiah as he claims, then let him save himself."

Jesus, His body racked with pain, looked down at a middle-aged woman in black. Her head was lowered—trembling and weeping bitterly, she struggled to find the strength to meet His eyes.

"Woman," He began, offering comfort. She looked up, tears streaming. "Behold your son." With a subtle nod He indicated a young man in blue robes who stood just a few feet away. The man approached, went to the woman's side, and placed a tender arm around her.

Mary, Paradine knew.

"John, behold your mother," the brutalized man said, the words soft.

Paradine looked on in astonishment.

He's dying a horrific death, and He's concerned for her!

"I will see to her every need for the rest of my days," the blue-robed man promised.

Mary stepped forward. The centurion, realizing the woman was Jesus' mother, allowed her to walk right up to the base of the cross. She kissed her quivering fingertips, then reached up and gently touched the side of the crucified man's foot—carefully, so as not to cause Him added pain. Her touch lingered there.

"From before Your birth, I have loved You," she whispered.

A slight smile broke over the lips of her son. Paradine knew why.

She did not merely feel a mother's love for her child.

She believed.

With a final nod, the young man and the older woman turned and walked away, headed toward the downhill path. Paradine watched them go. Soon, they vanished through the gates of the city.

No one remained on the crest of Golgotha who bore sympathy for the proclaimed Messiah.

It came noon. The winds ceased and went deathly still. A viscous darkness descended, even more dense than that in the valley of the Welakiutl. Some groped their way along, fearing they had gone blind, while others sought a natural explanation for the phenomenon and chalked it up to a prolonged eclipse—merely a coincidental one, to be sure.

Paradine lowered himself to the ground, his eyes finding nothing around him. For more than an hour he sat, struggling to devise a way out, knowing his life rapidly was drawing to a close.

His life, and those of his beloved wife and son.

All control over his life had been wrested from him. He felt trapped, as if bound at the bottom of the sea. Engulfed by lethal pressure and cut off from all light and all hope, his brilliant mind could formulate no solution to the quandary forced upon him. There was no way out.

Except one.

A fateful choice was made.

"Can you hear me?" he said in his mind.

"We can," came the voices.

"You promise my wife and son will be safe?" he asked again. "If I agree?"

"They will not come to harm. You have our word."

A deep breath, and a pause.

"Then do it," Paradine decided, giving himself over to them. "Come into me."

"Once this journey of shadows has ended, we shall," they said, the words a chorus of joy. *"Your life has but begun, Daniel Paradine."*

A thrill filled him, tightening his chest, burning deep. The faces of his family hung before him.

Lisabeth. . .Michael. . .we're safe!

Also within his mind, less noble thoughts ignited. There, dim but growing brighter, tumbled a montage of the apparent future—power, wealth, women, and life eternal!

Who better to live forever than I? Think of the wonders I'll accomplish!

For three hours the sudden and total midnight lingered. Lamps were lit in the city below, but their light barely penetrated the gloom.

Paradine's thoughts had left the crucified men behind him. He could think only of himself, of the potential his immortality would hold.

Just imagine!

Finally, the darkness lifted. As quickly as it had fallen, it was gone.

The teacher looked over his shoulder. He saw at once that the hours had taken a toll upon the dying trio.

The man on the left hung limply, racked by occasional spasms. The man on the right, using the darkness, apparently had tried in vain to pull himself free, worsening the bleeding of his wrist and foot wounds. Large, wet blotches darkened his fore-arms, his feet, and the cross to which he was affixed.

Paradine had seen enough blood.

He turned away, thought for a moment, then out of simple respect rose to his feet. Reluctantly, he turned his attention to the man on the middle cross.

Jesus, it was obvious, had suffered most. The ground beneath Him was soaked a dark red. His shoulders and elbows, contorted and swollen, clearly had been dislocated. He had gone pale despite the contusions that marred Him almost from head to toe. His eyes remained wide, clearly signaling that, in the midst of the darkness, He had experienced an unimaginable horror.

What happened? wondered Paradine. *What did you see?*

"My God!" the man suddenly cried out, the words seemingly etched by torment. "My God! Why have You forsaken Me?"

A few arrogant chuckles rose from the much relieved onlookers.

"So, we learn the truth, after all," commented one. "He *is* a false prophet."

"Forsaken, and rightfully so!" said another. "That's the first time he hasn't dared to call the Lord his 'father.' Ha!"

"He's calling for Elijah to save him!" one shouted, having misunderstood the Aramaic cry of 'Eloi, Eloi.' "

No, Paradine remembered. *He's not—*

"He can call all he wants," said the first man. "No one is coming for him."

Paradine stepped forward.

He's quoting Scripture. . .a prophecy that foretold this very moment!

Utter astonishment gripped him. He found it hard to breathe.

The words of Gorgathuus reached into his mind, rising from the trees below.

"The Nazarene fool!" the hidden monster laughed. "Dying for a tyrant who has abandoned him! His God has turned his back, just as he did with the Flood, and with Samson, and at Aphek, and in this very city five centuries ago!"

Paradine could not tear his eyes away.

Jesus. . .!

Other voices finally drew Paradine's attention. There, well behind the crosses and unnoticed by most, four soldiers were casting lots onto the rocky soil, with the man's clothing as the stakes. They had divided most of His garments evenly among themselves, but were gambling to see who would claim His tunic, an item of rare quality.

Seamless, it had been woven in one piece.

Like the Bible. . .so many threads, forming a flawless whole.

"Oh, please," Gorgathuus scoffed. "It is a tale told by an

idiot, full of sound and fury, signifying nothing."

No, it isn't!

Jesus dropped his head, crimson sweat dripping from His face and hair. His raspy voice cut into the air. "I thirst. . ."

One of the bystanders hurried to a jar of vinegar that rested alongside the baskets containing the executioners' hammers and nails. He took a sponge, soaked it, and attached it to the tip of a long, straight branch. Smiling, he returned to the cross and lifted it to Jesus' lips.

"How thirsty are you?" he said scornfully. "Enough for this?"

His battered face wrenched into a grimace, the crucified king took a bit of the sour wine into His mouth, but it did nothing to alleviate His thirst. Turning away, He closed his eyes and dropped His head, visibly struggling to breathe.

The onlooker chuckled, withdrew the sponge, and tossed it aside.

"I suppose not," he laughed. "Let's see if Elijah *does* come to his rescue. . .that's about all the hope he has left."

For more than six hours, Paradine had stood on the hilltop. Gorgathuus would not let him leave, not until the deed was done. During that time, many things had filled the teacher's mind, things he had refused to hear before, things his wife and others so often had told him.

He felt tremendous empathy for the crucified men—even their breathing was a torture now, each exhalation an agony, and the sound alone was excruciating for him.

Heavily burdened with his own guilt, he had kept his distance much of the time, his eyes averted from their sufferings. But suddenly, he was drawn irresistibly forward, like nothing he had felt before. Something new stirred within him.

Step after measured step he approached. He came to a halt

within the shadow of the central cross, so close he could have reached out to touch it.

Jesus lifted His head slightly. Unblinking, He looked directly into Paradine's eyes.

A deep chill swept through the teacher. He took a few steps back.

The Man's gaze followed him.

He sees me! How can it be?

A voice spoke within Paradine's heart. Finally, he heard.

Finally, he listened.

Jesus closed His eyes. Paradine turned away, overwhelmed and openly weeping.

After a few moments, a final utterance came from the lips of the Son of the living God.

"It. . .is done."

His head dropped lifelessly onto His chest.

A laugh rose in Paradine's ears. His cheeks still wet, he turned to see Gorgathuus crouched low in the distance, just beyond the hilltop.

"The man who would be God," the beast chuckled, "now just so much meat and bone, hung on a tree. There will be no Elijah today, coming down with clouds and fire." He turned, still laughing, and began downhill.

But His would not be the last word.

A promise had been kept.

Upheaval wrenched the world as the ancient barrier crumbled. The ground shook violently beneath Paradine's feet, throwing him backward, off balance. His searching feet slipped on the crumbling edge of the plateau, and suddenly nothing but air was beneath them.

He fell. The plunge went on and on—

Then, with no jolting impact, he was on solid ground inside the mountain cavern. Vertigo momentarily overcame him, and just as quickly subsided. The blue glow ebbed to amber.

"Impressive, was it not?" the thing crowed. *"Truly, you have witnessed but a portion of our greatness. . .but what we have shown you was wondrous enough."*

"Yes," Paradine said. "It made quite an impression."

"Tell us. . .what most struck awe within your heart? The conquering of kingdoms? The glory of battle? The cunning of this great mind?"

"The death of one innocent Man," said the scholar. "Nothing else you showed me made any difference."

The beast roared and exploded from its throne. In an instant, Paradine was pinned against the icy floor, the nightmare crouching over him. Its cold burned against his flesh.

"You saw wonders men would give their lives to see! You learned secrets they would kill to know!"

"You have a very high opinion of yourself," Paradine stammered in fear.

"You are not the man we thought you were! You are common and ignorant, like all the others! We are finished with you!"

It lifted a clawed hand high into the air, as if to bring it down in a lethal, eviscerating blow. Paradine helplessly wrenched his eyes shut.

A moment passed. Then another.

He dared to look.

The thing stood upright over him, its upper body shaking, its expression one of confusion and panic. It no longer seemed concerned with the man on the floor. It clutched its head and staggered backward.

"NO!" it cried out, the sound shaking the walls. Ice dust and debris rained down.

235

The thing trembled fiercely, toppling against its grisly throne. *"You must not do this! You cannot do this!"*

A motion appeared, surrounding it, a swirling cloud of light that was diaphanous at first but grew more dense and more rapid with each passing second. A rush of wind filled the cave. Paradine crawled backward until he could go no farther, then braced himself against a pile of bones and managed to stagger to his feet.

The cloud became a cocoon of violence, enveloping the thing until its dark form no longer could be seen. A clawed hand momentarily protruded from the cyclone as if reaching for help. Then another. Both quickly disappeared as the roar of the flow became intolerable. Paradine covered his ears but could not take his eyes from the sight. Bones clattered all around him before being swept up to become deadly missiles. The temperature plummeted, and frost appeared on his hair and face. He pushed back, nestled into a shallow crevice in the wall, and hung on, hoping it would provide a measure of protection. He eyed the exit tunnel—no way to reach it, not now. The projectiles repeatedly struck him, and he began to notice they were not all made of bone.

Please. . .not the swords!

The treasure pile, far from the center of the storm, had begun to yield to the winds, but thus far only its smaller items had become airborne. His ears still covered, Paradine huddled against the storm and attempted to shield his whitened face with his forearms. As his eyes kept closing reflexively against the icy maelstrom, he fought not to lose sight of the whirlwind's core.

The beast screamed, the sound louder and more terrifying than anything Paradine yet had heard. It rose above the din of the wind, a solitary shriek of death.

"Why have you forsaken me. . . ?"

The winds finally began to die down. The glowing funnel

narrowed. Skulls and femurs, vertebrae and ribs, coins and gem-stones all slowed in their flight and clattered to the floor. Paradine saw the cloud take on a different shape as it broke from a single mass into many.

They—the possessing spirits—were separating before his eyes.

Paradine stood fully erect and lowered his arms. Before him, faces began to appear, connected to ethereal bodies that wisped away into nothingness. They were beautiful, something from a dream. Enthralled, he watched them as they moved, their grace far beyond that of any earthly dance. There were more of them than he could begin to count—more, it seemed, than could possibly fill the space they occupied.

"How many are you?" he managed to ask.

"We are a hundred thousand," came the music. *"And more."*

Like an army they began to draw ranks, their forms still indistinct. Hair like spun diamond rose from their heads, flowing as if on rising currents of air. Their faces were lovely, their eyes sparkling.

The cold was numbing, the stench unbearable.

Then, as Paradine stood looking them in the eyes, they rushed forward en masse. Holding his breath, he braced himself against the cavern wall, his face turned aside.

The impact knocked the wind out of him.

Something hurled the demons violently backward, as if repulsed. The man they sought to possess had become like a brick wall to them, rigid and impenetrable. As Paradine stood gasping for air, he saw them regroup, their eyes now cold and black, their faces hollow and inhuman. Their anger burned.

"Liar!" they screeched in unison. The hideous sound cut through Paradine like breaking glass. *"You have betrayed us! You are not the empty house you were!"*

Paradine, caught off guard, ran a cautious hand along his chest and stomach as slowly he regained his breath.

"We cannot enter! The other has taken you! How did we not know? How did we not know?"

"'Other?'"

"At the cross!" they shrieked. *"At the cross! His blood has sealed you! Closed you to us! It cannot be! We were listening! We were listening!"*

"Listening?"

"Your thoughts were ours! We would have known! We would have known!"

Paradine watched in terror as they encompassed him like hungry wolves.

"You will die for your treachery! We shall find another, and through him, you and your family will die!"

"I don't understand—"

"Liar! Liar! We will destroy you!"

"No," came a voice that was both loud and fearless. "You will not."

All eyes in the cavern swung toward the tunnel entrance. There stood Lucky, his arms extended toward the spirits, his rifle clutched sideways in widespread hands as if it were a talisman.

"Get out of here!" Paradine warned him, fearful the man would be possessed. "You don't know what these things will do!"

"I know what they will *not* do," Lucky said, his eyes still fixed upon the demonic legion.

The spirits screamed and recoiled from the frontiersman, their eyes burning a vivid red.

"You will not stop us!" they threatened.

"I won't," Lucky agreed, "but He who made you *will*."

"NO!"

"In the name of Jesus, you will inhabit no other living thing, now or ever. . . ."

Their screams were loud and shrill.

"You will wander the waterless places, where you will find no rest and no comfort will be given you! All with the breath of life are closed to you, now and forever, and no flesh will you take as a refuge!"

"Leave us desolate," they hissed, *"and we will go forth, filling the earth, turning man against man and brother against brother! Their blood will flow in great rivers, and the fallen will cover the land!"*

The frontiersman did not waver.

"No harbor shall be given you! So says the One who is the blessed and only Sovereign, the King of kings and Lord of lords!"

"NO—!"

The spirits rushed forward. Instantly, a brilliant white light flared into being, filling the cave.

Paradine covered his eyes. He heard something like the sounds of battle, a cacophony of clashing swords and screams of fury. He tried to steal a glance at the unearthly conflict, but the glare was too intense. All he could do was drop to the floor and huddle low, hoping to stay out of the way.

Then, in a moment, it ended. All went still.

Paradine lifted his head to find the light still emanating from the tunnel, but more dimly now. He saw a figure in the midst of the light, one of astounding beauty. He shuddered and covered his head, fearful of its presence.

"Look at me," the figure said. "Don't be afraid."

Paradine again raised his eyes. Still the radiance was there but at a tolerable level, the only light in the chamber. The ocher glow that once had spilled from the walls was gone.

He slowly rose, leaning on the wall in order to find his feet.

His legs quivered like jelly beneath him. His heart flung itself hard against his rib cage.

The being before him stood eight feet tall, clothed in flowing robes of brilliant white. It was girded at the waist with a wide belt of gold, and in its right hand it held a bladed thing of dazzling metal, which once had borne the appearance of a rifle.

"Who are you?" Paradine asked, his voice breaking. "What happened to—?"

"It still is I, my friend."

"*Lucky?*"

"Lukanya." He smiled. "I am one who serves the Lord. And truth be told, there is no such thing as *luck.*"

"An *angel?*"

"Yes, Daniel."

"And the *whole* time, you were—"

"I've waited here, in this place of darkness. . .waited for you, and for the fulfillment of what was to be."

"Which was. . . ?"

"The end of the long and horrible reign of Gorgathuus, and the deliverance of one Daniel Paradine."

"What happened?" the rattled teacher asked. "I mean, I had agreed to let them come into me, but. . ."

"They could not," the angel said. "You are not your own."

"What?"

"There, at the base of the cross, you *believed*. You are His, as was to be from the beginning. You received Him, openly and willingly."

"Yes." Paradine nodded, recalling the moment his heart had opened. "I did. . ."

"And from that moment, you were no longer empty. Another Spirit now fills you, and through Him you will become what you were destined to be. You have been bought at a great price. . . never forget that."

And then, with a fading of light, the frontiersman once more stood before him. Only the meager light of Paradine's toppled lantern bathed the cavern.

He picked up the lamp and approached his friend. "Were you one of those who died here, in this valley?"

"No, no," Lucky said gently. "Men and angels are two very different things, and always have been. Just as you were created human, we were created angels. . .but we assume different outward appearances as are required for the task at hand. We have served our Creator since before your world was made, and will do so even after everything takes place on earth that is to take place."

"So, when you said you came in *over* the mountains. . ."

A mischievous smile crossed the angel's face as he scratched his beard.

"Yes, Daniel."

Paradine glanced around the chamber, then past the angel, down the curving tunnel.

"The demons. . .where did they go?"

"Into the world. They will possess no one, but they remain free to wander, and to conspire, and to whisper."

"Why?"

"It's a part of what must be."

Paradine looked down at the place where Gorgathuus had last stood. There, upon the slowly melting ice, a huge, deformed skeleton lay crumpled amid a pile of ashen dust. Every bone was diseased and misshapen, warped and covered in knots and protrusions. Each provided dramatic evidence of the centuries of possession the former man had suffered.

"What happened to *him?*"

241

"It was they who sustained him. Once they departed his body, he reverted to that which he should have been long ago, if not for their influence."

"They wanted to enter into me. They said I'd live forever. . . ."

"And you *will*," Lucky said, "but eternal life comes only from God. Had *their* will been done instead, you would have suffered the same corruption as Gorgathuus. All that they told you were lies, for they serve the father of lies, in whom there is no truth."

Paradine's head swam with questions.

"What happened? I mean, when I was on Golgotha. . ." He choked up. "He *saw* me."

"Yes, He did," smiled the frontiersman. "There is no place you can go that is beyond His reach, not even the inner mind of such a one as Gorgathuus. You weren't truly in the past. . .you had not traveled in time. But He came to where you were, and met you *there,* as He always has with all who are His."

"I was His?" Paradine wondered. "But I never believed. . .not before today."

"You have been His since before the foundations of the universe were laid. All unfolds as God has determined it will. Those who are His hear His call at the time and place of His choosing, and not a moment before."

"Why didn't the demons know? Why didn't Gorgathuus? When I was standing before the cross, and Jesus looked into my eyes and I heard His voice, I answered Him. Why wasn't I overheard?"

"You were shielded from them. They thought they still had access to your thoughts, but they did not. In the same manner that the demons shielded you from Gorgathuus in hopes of deceiving him, we shielded you from them all, that they would not learn too quickly that you had received Christ."

"But all the horrible things I saw. . .the people who died. . ."

"All is used by God for good, even the worst His creatures can conceive to do. Mankind turned from Him at the outset, and since has suffered the painful consequences inherent in such a separation. But their reclamation has been provided for, through Jesus Christ, and that which you witnessed due to Gorgathuus's intense pride ultimately brought you to Him. . . and through you, many others will be saved."

Paradine was surprised by that. "What? Others? I don't understand."

"You will," said Lucky. "And very soon."

"My wife," Paradine hoped. "My son. . ."

The angel smiled widely. "They are well. They are waiting."

Paradine's vision blurred, curtained by tears.

"I was so afraid. . .I thought for sure that Gorgathuus or the demons within him would find them and. . ."

"They could not have taken a life that belonged to Jesus. You saw that in the valley. . .a wife spared where a husband was not, and not a child died. Even in the cemetery, where some graves were violated by the beast while others were not. . .the believers' mortal remains weren't his to touch."

"But, the thing Gorgathuus had become seemed so powerful. . . ."

"Powerful, yes. Do not underestimate the strength or intellect of the enemy. But this is not a matter of good and evil being equal—but opposite. God the father remains sovereign in all things. You have been bought at a great price, and you belong to the enemy no more."

Paradine, tears streaming, lowered his head and offered a brief, silent, and awkward prayer of thanks.

"I'm not too good at that," he said, wiping his eyes. "Not

enough practice, I guess."

"No man knows how to pray as he should," Lucky said. "But the Holy Spirit, who now lives within you, intercedes with groanings too deep for words. It is the *heart* that God hears."

"I remember reading that," Paradine said. "The book of Romans, I think."

"Indeed. You have quite a head start through your knowledge of Scripture."

Paradine recalled the many times he had leafed through those pages, the hours he had spent studying them as if they held no special value, as if they ranked no higher than the other writings of man.

"Before," he said, "they were just words. Dead words written by dead people. . .dry, meaningless history. Do's and don'ts I didn't much care for. But now, it's different. . ."

"My time here is finished," Lucky said. "Farewell, my friend. I will never forget your kindness."

"Me? What did *I* do?"

"You gave bread and meat to a stranger when you had little to spare. And you worried more for my life than your own."

Paradine was humbled. "I just did what anyone would have done."

"No." The angel smiled. "You did not. I have visited many, and those such as you have been few."

Paradine extended a hand. Lucky took it.

"Thank you," the teacher said. "For everything."

With a final smile and a wink, Lucky was gone. Paradine detected a glow coming from the tunnel. He started toward it, his boots kicking aside scattered bones and shattered treasures.

With one step a familiar noise rang out. He glanced down, spied the source of the sound, and bent to pick it up. After a moment of awed contemplation, he slipped the object into his coat pocket and continued on.

The light ahead grew brighter. As he rounded the final curve, he learned why. His heart leapt.

The valley was bathed in full morning light—the first it had seen in the better part of a century.

Chapter 14

Paradine stood at the mouth of the cave, laughing and crying. For the first time, he beheld the valley in its totality.

From his high vantage point, he could see it all. The lake, the Indian village, the forests of firs and cedars, and the vast clearing beyond.

He gasped, striving to grasp the enormity of the sight.

Wagons. Hundreds of them.

They littered the periphery of the meadow floor, piled in crude heaps against the rising mountains as if shoved out of the way. It was like a vast Sargasso Sea of prairie schooners, lost and forgotten and left to decay.

So that's how he did it.

Gorgathuus had kept the area just within the entrance pass clear. Once he had murdered and destroyed each wagon train, he cast all traces of their presence aside so that the next group of pioneers to enter the valley would suspect nothing before it was too late.

Paradine quickly spotted his own wagon. Of the twelve that had made up his group, it alone remained intact. Straining his eyes to the limit, he tried to discern anyone or anything moving in the valley, but saw nothing.

One sight thrilled him. The pass through which they had entered was there again, just beyond the camp. He wondered if perhaps, somehow, it always had been.

Hurriedly, he made his way down the mountainside, thrilling at the sight of his shadow. All around him, the grasses and frost-coated rocks were beginning to thaw beneath the rays of the sun. The lake still shone white—frozen to its bottom, it would take much longer to return to normal.

A warm, gentle breeze swept through. The sights, the sounds, and the wind in his hair—the valley seemed like an entirely different place to him now, as if he were entering it for the first time.

He reached the bottom of the hill, cut through a narrow band of forest, and broke into a dead run across the fields. His eyes were fixed on Seukani's house, which he now saw was one of ten that stood in two rows on the lake's southwestern shore. The totems rose there as well, tall and noble and proud, a testament to the skill of their makers.

A few animal carcasses littered the hunting grounds—oxen mostly, perhaps even Paradine's own. All had been largely devoured.

He sprang up to the old man's door and threw it open with only the barest knock.

"Seukani!" he called, bursting into the room. "The sun! We're free!"

There came no reply.

Fearfully, he left the house and headed toward the southern forest, beyond which lay his campsite. His eyes constantly scanned the woods for any sight of Seukani and for others who might have survived, others who had lived to see the sunrise.

He broke through the tree line and into the meadow at the end of the valley. At once, in the distance, he saw his wagon amid the others of their train, small but growing nearer. To his right lay the graveyard, which now appeared to him in its entirety.

It was vast. A hundred markers rose there, perhaps more.

After another minute, he was at his wagon. He took a quick look inside but found it unoccupied.

"Lisabeth!" he called out, turning in different directions. "Michael!"

No reply.

He circled the camp until he faced an area where he had not previously ventured. "Lisabeth! Michael! Can you hear me?!"

Only the wind answered him.

Returning to his wagon, he leaned in enough to pull his water bottle from its place. It was almost empty, depleted during his first visit with Lucky. As he tipped it up to draw the last remaining drops, he heard a sound.

Voices—and the two most wonderful words he had ever heard.

"Daniel!"

"Daddy!"

He spun and looked to the west. There, beyond the cemetery, two dozen people were headed in his direction. In the lead were his wife and son.

249

The bottle fell to the ground.

He took off at full speed, never looking away for fear of losing them again. The final hundred feet shrank to nothing.

They fell into each other's arms, kissing and embracing each other. He squeezed Lisabeth and felt Michael's arms around his waist.

"Oh, Daniel," Lisabeth wept, "I thought we'd lost you. . . ."

"I told you," he said, burying his emotions behind a subtle smile, "you're not getting rid of me that easily."

After another deep kiss, he knelt and enfolded his son in his arms.

"I'm so proud of you," he said to the boy, "taking such good care of your mother."

"I had some help," Michael said. "From the other man."

"Who? What other man?"

Another voice cried out.

"Mr. Paradine!"

The teacher looked up to see Captain Wills approaching, his arm in a sling.

"Captain," he smiled, "good to see you."

"What happened? What did you find out there? How did you—?"

"It's a long story," Paradine smiled, shaking his hand. "Covers a few thousand years, actually. I'll tell you about it after we get out of this place."

He looked at the others, none of whom seemed the worse for wear. Marjorie Carter, Harvey Langtree, Ben and Eliza May Taylor and their daughters, Billy Lassiter, and nine other children, all of whom, sadly, had now been orphaned.

One other figure approached, his face bearing not a smile but a look of shame.

"John," Paradine said, spying Forrester, who brought up the rear.

"Dan," the man began, eyes down. "I'm so glad you're okay. I don't know what to say. . . . I left you alone out there, and. . ."

"It's all right." Paradine reached out and gripped the man's shoulder. "Where I went, I had to go alone. You couldn't have come with me. Your place was to stay with Seukani."

Forrester smiled, relieved a bit but still feeling guilt. "Speaking of whom," he said, "he was with us for a while. Back there, in the cave. But when the sun came up, he took off. . .headed back to his house, I guess."

"I'll look in on him." Paradine smiled. "Thanks."

The group returned to the wagons and began to assess the work that lay ahead in preparation for leaving. Paradine stood at his wife's side, and for a moment they watched as the children, Michael included, played tag in the open meadow.

"Daniel," she asked, caressing his face, "where are your glasses?"

"First," he said, "tell me what happened after I went to look for Michael. Where were you the whole time?"

"Something attacked the camp," she said. "Weren't many of us left by then. We fled into the darkness and got separated almost immediately. I was too afraid to call out. Just wandered a bit, hoping to bump into something or someone I knew. . .and terrified I'd be found by whatever was killing us." She looked into the distance. "Then, this frontiersman found me. . ."

Paradine smiled. "We met."

"Did you? Why didn't he tell me that?"

"I'm sure he had his reasons."

"He led me back that way. . ." She pointed toward the western edge of the valley, where the mountains rose and wagons were piled high. "Sure knew his way around in the dark. We weaved through the wagons and came to a cave entrance buried beneath them. Hidden by them. He kept going out and coming back, and one by one, he brought us there. Hid us from whatever it was that was attacking us. It was a big cavern, with a warm fire, and food and water. I kept asking about you, if he'd seen you, but all he'd say was that he was sure you'd be safe.

"And then, after a while, he told us to stay put, and he left. Said he had something he had to go take care of, and we'd know when it was safe to leave. So we waited, and. . ."

She turned her eyes upward, into the clear blue sky. Again she embraced her husband, holding him tight, her head pressed against his shoulder.

". . .and it was a miracle," she said, her eyes wet. "I couldn't believe it. The sun rose."

He held her, feeling her warmth against him, knowing at long last they were out of harm's way.

"Yes," Paradine smiled, closing his eyes in thanks. *He did.*

◉ ◉ ◉

A thousand memories washed over Seukani. He stood before his home of more than sixty years, gazing into the blue expanse above, his mind filled with distant images. It was just as he remembered—the sun against his face and hands, the kiss of the breeze, the sound of the wind in the branches. Gone were the songs of the birds and the calls of the animals that had lived there in that long-ago paradise. He mourned their loss.

Hobbling on his malformed foot, he reached the nearest of the totems. He placed a hand against it, finally feeling the warmth of summer wood once more.

Father. . .Mother. . .the spirits have remembered us, he said inwardly, addressing his ancestors as he often did. *Chayatocha no longer rules here. At last, he is no more. . .but his end was not brought about by those we thought we knew.*

He smiled, still barely able to believe it.

Last night. . .I walked with a spirit.

The morning sky looked down upon a faithful man, wounded from birth, who had finally been set free.

◎ ◎ ◎

"Parlez vous Francais?" called a familiar voice from nearby.

Seukani turned to see Paradine approaching, a wide smile on the man's face.

"Oui." The Indian grinned, taking a few steps toward him. Paradine looked into the aged face as they drew closer and saw something new there.

Hope.

They came together, and the man from Ohio embraced the last of the Welakiutl. They stood together, side by side, and shared a quiet moment.

"I have longed for this," the old man said. "And now that it has come, it is as a dream."

"I think I know how you feel," Paradine said.

Minutes passed in silence. Time grew short.

"Listen," he began, "we're about to head out. My wagon's in fine shape. We managed to find enough living oxen out wandering around to make a good sized team, and got them hitched up. Dug what supplies we could out of what's left of the other wagons. We should be all right."

The white-headed man nodded slightly.

"We're going back out, to meet up with the trail again. If we're lucky, we'll reach Saraleah inside of a month."

There's no such thing as luck, Paradine remembered, once the word had passed his lips.

"I want you to come with us," he continued. "Please don't stay here alone. I know it's your village, and I know you've lived here all your life. . .but I think it's time you knew friends and family again. *My* family."

Seukani glanced around, at the lake, the totems, the trees, the mountains.

"This is the land of my people," he said. "It has always been so. Never did we leave. Never was there a need to."

Paradine took a deep breath, accepting the old man's gentle refusal.

Well, I tried—

A twinkle shone in the old man's eye.

"There is a place, however," he said, "that I have always wanted to see. . .a beautiful place I once was told about."

"Where is that?" a delighted Paradine asked.

"Have you heard of. . .Trois-Rivières?"

Epilogue

From the diary of Daniel Paradine, May 17, 1861:

Of the fifty-three who entered the valley on that fateful day, twenty-one of us survived.

It has been nearly four years since the events that now mark the turning point in all our lives. Barely have I spoken of it—nor has my wife, or any of the rest of those who shared in the horror of those few days. Michael, who turned twelve this past tenth of March, still has nightmares of our ordeal, but thankfully they have lessened both in frequency and intensity over time.

But now, with the portentous events of the last few months, the time has come to set down these words. I do not relish the thought of revisiting our interrupted journey—its more grisly images have haunted me quite enough.

The morning of our departure, we searched the valley for any sign of other survivors. We were not hopeful, and as time slipped away and our calls went unanswered, our hopes diminished further. A few were found dead, and we buried them there in the graveyard begun by those who in the past had fallen prey to Gorgathuus. I did not tell the others of the ghastly remains that filled the thing's lair, inasmuch as it would accomplish nothing and serve only to intensify the horror of the fates our friends had met. Better they be remembered as they walked in life, and not for the manner in which they perished.

We were delighted to find so many of our oxen still alive as we searched the valley. Had there been none remaining, our journey back to the trail might well have been impossible. Eight were found, and with a modicum of effort we were able to yoke them to my wagon, which alone the beast had left untouched. A check of the remaining wagons yielded sufficient food, water, and other supplies, and by noon we were ready to depart.

My last stop before our exodus was the home of Seukani, who I had prayed would consent to join us. I knew it was asking a lot of him to leave behind everything he had known, but after the years he had spent so terrified and alone, he was willing to do so. These last four years, he has been a special delight for me.

We made good time in heading back, and by sunset we reached the trail. Providence had placed another wagon train but a quarter mile along, which had stopped for the night and was in the midst of preparing supper. We were welcomed by the group and readily agreed to travel with their party.

The remainder of our journey westward was blessedly uneventful, and upon reaching Oregon City we reluctantly went our separate ways. The shared experience had made us a family in a very real sense, and the sense of loss we felt as we parted was heartfelt.

Captain Wills, having received medical attention, headed south toward Sacramento and the business interests that awaited him. Marjorie Carter accompanied him there, but will not remain in California—widowed on our journey, she did not wish to live so far removed from her loved ones. Understandably, she did not wish to see a wagon train ever again, and intended to await the coming of the railroad before heading back. Since their departure, we have received word from neither she nor the good captain, but I pray that both are safe and well.

The Taylors moved on to Portland, but not before adopting Billy Lassiter, who had lost both parents in the span of a single day, as their own. Most of the remaining children found homes with relatives, and it is my understanding that those who lived briefly in the Oregon City orphanage have since been placed with loving families.

Upon our arrival in Saraleah, we found a small, tightly knit community that welcomed us with open doors and open arms. They are a gentle, sharing lot, and remind both Lisabeth and me of the friends we left behind.

We found our new house waiting for us, fully furnished and wanting only for a family to make it their own. There was a final bit of work to be done, though, before I allowed Lisabeth to see it. After receiving the help of a few neighbors, I brought her to a yellow house with white trim, a white picket fence, a stone walk, and flower beds overflowing with yellow daisies. I love her so much—why God saw fit to bless such a prideful man with such a wonderful woman, I'll never know.

Upon our arrival, the schoolhouse was nearing completion

and the neighboring church stood without a pastor. I offered my services and found the town council more than receptive. So, in addition to being the town's first schoolteacher, I am also its first clergyman. With God's help, this growing congregation will keep its pathway straight and always glorify Him.

The school library has been a great success, with many books shipped in from down the coast having been added to my own. The children here are bright and voracious learners, and with few exceptions are remarkably well behaved.

John Forrester, in search of a new beginning, settled here in Saraleah. Within a week, he met a lovely young woman named Rebecca Heald, whose family originally had come from Michigan. The mayor, delighted with the prospect of having a practicing dentist in town, spoke with him about setting up an office—and in no time, it seemed, John was busy seeing patients. I myself needed to have some dental work done just this past year, and by golly if the nitrous oxide John told me about isn't all he said it was. The continued advancements of science never cease to amaze me, and I can only wonder what the future holds. One is hard-pressed to envision any future innovations—what else possibly could be brought into our daily lives?

I am also happy to note that John has come back to the Lord. The loss of his beloved first wife drove him into great despair, into depths from which he no longer could see God—but what a blessed thing it is that our Creator is merciful and patient! Though John lost his faith for a time, his Lord remained faithful throughout and lovingly embraced him once more.

Which brings me to Seukani.

On our journey westward, I spoke with him at length about what had happened in the cave. I was surprised to learn that the angel had revealed himself to the old man, shortly before the destruction of Gorgathuus. Seukani, with such a blessing imparted, was hungry to know more about a God who loved him so, who did not deal with men based upon whim or efforts at appeasement. Each day of our last month on the trail, I read to him from the Bible, translating the passages to the best of my ability into French. Like a sponge he absorbed it all, listening and asking questions. I did my best to provide answers, and in many cases, we learned together. As I read those pages for the first time with open eyes, it was as if every page was new. Before, I merely had known *of* God. Now, I *knew* Him.

Less than a year after our arrival here, I baptized my Indian friend in the Willamette River. He chose to remain in this town and has become one of its most beloved citizens. Though his age and increasing frailty would never allow such a trip, he still dreams of visiting Canada one day, though he never has told me the reason why. Whenever I ask, he just gets a glint in his eye and smiles quietly—I think it has become a game with him, and it's one I don't mind a bit.

I am fully and sometimes painfully aware of what it took for me to come to the realization of God's truth. Wretched man that I am—thinking myself wise, all along I was a fool. I, like Thomas, quite literally have seen and have believed.

Never will I forget what I saw on Golgotha. Those wounded eyes, as deep as all eternity, will stay with me forever. I feel as if a million words churn within me concerning the experience, yet at the same time those words could never properly express what I saw and heard and felt, there on that hilltop, before that cross. None of us will ever know, or *can* ever know, what Christ endured that day—we can only be grateful, and remember always the amazing grace that alone saves us.

As I write these words, as I live each day, I bear a constant token of the thing I met in that horrid cave—my clarity of vision, restored by the creature, still remains. Anytime I read a textbook or hymnal, or look clearly upon the faces of my family, I remember.

Upon my desk I keep something else carried with me from the cavern, a reminder of a different sort. It is an item of which I have spoken with no one but my wife—a small pouch of heavy blue fabric, fragile with age, containing the price once paid for the life of our Savior. I cannot look upon those thirty pieces of silver without wonder, without inwardly trembling, without being awed by the love of a God who died for those who did not love Him in return.

It truly is amazing how He transformed even the evils of Gorgathuus and Judas, forging from them, in part, the single greatest act of love in all of human history.

The climactic events in the thing's lair, I now fear, are coming to further fruition, and herein lies my impetus for putting down these words. We have become aware of actions taken elsewhere in this great nation, things which do not bode well for the future. South Carolina has seceded from the Union, and Ft. Sumter has been fired upon in the first act of what has become war.

Man needs little help in turning to hatred, and it now appears that the whisperings of the demonic hundreds of thousands were the final spark needed to ignite a great conflagration. Their promised threats are coming to pass.

"Man against man and brother against brother," they said.

I fear what further whisperings might bring, for in that cave I came to know too well the horrors of war. But I know through the words of Lukanya that what must take place indeed will—that God remains in control.

I pray that American blood will not flow as the demonic horde threatened it would. But whatever tomorrow holds, may the will of God be done.

And, in His grace, may He bless us all.

A Note from the Author

Day to day, I struggle with my own fallen nature, realizing that every sin, every defiance of the will of my Creator is a blow of the hammer, pounding into those nails, atop that ancient hill. I placed Him on that cross as surely as did the soldiers of Rome, for it was my sins for which He suffered and died. I know all too well the sorrow that tore at the apostle Paul, who understood that no man leaves sin fully behind until he has departed the earthly body of death that enshrouds him.

Yet, while we were still sinners, Christ died for us.

"For this I was born," He said.

Even in the midst of His suffering, He declared for all the world to hear that His ordeal on the cross was a fulfillment of ancient and incredibly specific prophecies:

I am poured out like water, and all my bones are out of joint: my heart is like wax; it is melted in the midst of my bowels. My strength is dried up like a potsherd; and my tongue cleaveth to my jaws; and thou hast brought me into the dust of death. For dogs have compassed me: the assembly of the wicked have inclosed me: they pierced my hands and my feet. I may tell all my bones: they look and stare upon me. They part my garments among them, and cast lots upon my vesture. . .

These words from the twenty-second Psalm, an exacting description of death by crucifixion, were set down centuries before such a form of punishment even existed. And no mere crucifixion, but His specifically—including events beyond His personal control.

And in crying out as He did, asking His Father why He had been forsaken, our Lord Jesus also revealed to us that, for that horrible interval upon the cross, God the Father indeed turned His back on His Son. Having placed the sins of us all on the precious shoulders of the sacrifice He provided, God could have no fellowship with the bearer of those sins until they had been paid for. I cannot imagine the depth of the pain, loneliness, and isolation Jesus must have felt—as He bore the grief and despair and guilt of billions, as He suffered more than any man ever to live, He also for the first time was separated from the remainder of the Godhead.

And that separation, while brief as man counts the hours, also is everlasting.

Our Creator surely exists outside of time, for its flow is a part of the universe He made, and nothing exists that He did not make. Therefore, for God, there is no passage of time—no past, no future.

There is only *now*.

Which means that, even as I write this, He hangs on that cross, bearing a burden that should be mine, laying down His life that I may live. For all eternity, as we measure things, He will endure that pain unceasingly and indeed always has. Never will it pass. Be mindful of this.

Shane Johnson
September 2003

Would you like to offer feedback on this novel?

Interested in starting a book discussion group?

Check out www.barbourbooks.com for
a *Reader Survey* and *Book Club Questions.*

SHANE JOHNSON, a writer, graphic artist and spaceflight historian, is author of the novels *The Last Guardian* (a 2002 Christy Award finalist and Booklist Top Ten selection for 2001), *ICE* (a 2003 Christy Award finalist), *Chayatocha* and the upcoming *A Form of Godliness.* He also served as producer/director for the video documentary *Apollo 13: Flight for Survival,* and was a design consultant for the award-winning HBO miniseries *From the Earth to the Moon.* Shane lives in Texas with his wife and son.

More information on the author can be found on the Internet at www.shanejohnsonbooks.com.

c.

The Dandelion Killer
ISBN 1-58660-753-7
A mentally handicapped man is
suspected of murder while his longtime
friend is threatened by the real killer.
Is she ready to face eternity?

Body Politic
ISBN 1-58660-600-X
Medical science and political
drama collide in this
"Grishamesque" thriller that
centers on fetal stem cell research.

Operation Firebrand: Crusade
ISBN 1-58660-676-X
When Muslim raiders destroy
a village in the south of Sudan,
the Firebrand team of Christian
commandos is sent into the breach.

The Crystal Cavern
ISBN 1-58660-767-7
Danger surrounds the icy Ozark hills when
Dr. Sable Chamberlin and Paul Murphy
go searching for a murderer's motive—and
discover that their names might be next to
appear in the obituaries.